THIRTEEN GHOST STORIES

First published in 2004 by

WOODFIELD PUBLISHING
Bognor Regis, West Sussex, England
www.woodfieldpublishing.com

© Alexander Kinghorn, 2004

ISBN 1-903953-54-5

THIRTEEN GHOST STORIES

ALEXANDER KINGHORN

Woodfield

- To my wife, Margaret -

Contents

Also by A.M Kinghorn

BARBOUR'S BRUCE
ed. for Saltire Classics, Oliver & Boyd (1960)

MEDIAEVAL DRAMA
Evans Bros, London (1968); 2nd edition Volturna Press (1983)

THE MIDDLE SCOTS POETS
Edward Arnold & Indiana University Press (1970)

THE CHORUS OF HISTORY Literary-Historical Relations in Renaissance
Britain 1485-1558
Blandford Press, London and Barnes & Noble, New York (1971)

POEMS BY ALLAN RAMSAY & ROBERT FERGUSSON
ed. with Alexander Law for the Scottish Academic Press, Edinburgh (1974)

THE WORKS OF ALLAN RAMSAY
ed. with Alexander Law *et al.* Blackwoods, for the Scottish Text Society,
Edinburgh & London, (6 vols, 1953-75)

SHAKESPEARE: THE MERCHANT OF VENICE, Macmillan (1988)

THE LIFE & DEATH OF MICHAEL X, UNI Books, Waterford (1981)
(issued under a pseudonym).

Professor Kinghorn has also been a contributor to:
   Modern Language Review;
   English Studies;
   Neophilologus
   Journal of European Studies;
   Scottish Literary Journal,
   English Miscellany
   and others.

Preface

Many authors associate creative inspiration with a real place, tracing it to a house or garden familiar from childhood or more rarely from the memory of a single visit. Dr M.R. James, doyen of ghost-story writers, drew attention to the suggestive importance of settings in a preface to his *Collected Ghost Stories* when he identified actual sites, coastal resorts, college libraries, cathedrals and crypts which he had adapted to create the unique atmosphere of eerie tension pervading his original tales.

In Professor Kinghorn's ghostly world, certain places, such as London's Wigmore Hall (called Woolgar Hall in the story) are easily identifiable; others, like 'Cwm Beris' in North Wales, are fictions. 'Kinlonie' and 'Monymuir' recall memories of the towns of Kintore and Alford in Aberdeenshire during the Second World War. An ancient 0-4-0 locomotive known as 'Meldrum Meggie' did exist and remained in shunting service until the 1930s. 'Bellucine Island' is an invention inspired by a cruise to the Caicos Islands in the Bahamas while 'Lacrasia' owes its inspiration to pre-independence Jamaica. The 'Ossian College' of 'The Window-Cleaner's Tale' is King's College in the University of Aberdeen. The Hallow House of 'Brotherly Love' has not yet been built, but Gil's Hill lies near the village of Bourn in Cambridgeshire. The popular resort of Briscombe in 'Elfride Awaits' bears some resemblance to the Cinque Port of Hythe in East Kent, but the archaeologist must seek in vain for Ruach among the conical mounds of Anglesey or for the Reverend Evan Partridge's *Early History of Mona*. 'Morton Barracks' disguises the wartime Baron's Hill Camp in Beaumaris, long since demolished, but those who have a mind to visit the *Catacombe Cappuccini* outside Palermo may see the vaults where clothed skeletons of long-dead Sicilians are preserved for the still-living to behold and where the superbly-embalmed body of the infant Rosalia Lombardo is displayed under glass.

Some decriers may claim that ghosts do not care to appear in cemeteries or in daylight but the Rose Garden of a crematorium not far from Brighton seems to have attracted a Phantom Beloved even in the heat of a summer afternoon. With some exceptions the supernatural agents in these stories are potentially hostile to the still-living, though in some instances it is arguable that their ill-will may be attributed as much to the narrator's mental state as to the malevolence of ghoulish revengers.

A.M.K.

About the Author

Professor A.M. Kinghorn is a widely-travelled academic whose collection of supernatural tales, his first incursion into fiction, reflects his catholic interests. Educated at the Universities of Aberdeen and Pembroke College, Cambridge, he served with the Intelligence Corps in post-war Vienna and subsequently held academic appointments in the United States, Canada, the West Indies, Denmark and the Middle East.

Professor Kinghorn retired in 1987 and now lives in Sandwich, Kent.

The cover illustration is from a photograph of the parish church of St Andrew in Sempringham, Lincs.

1. *The Girl with the Flaxen Hair*

"There was a man dwelt by a churchyard" is the first and last line of a ghost story in Shakespeare's *Winter's Tale*. I have myself never dwelt by a churchyard but my comfortable rented flat lay within a short walking distance of an active crematorium. Ghosts are not readily associated with crematoria but Shakespeare's tantalizing opening has connections, even with such a hygienic modern method of corpse disposal.

Now to my own Summer's Tale, a ghost story which began as a love story and in a way ended as one...

In the vanished world just before the Second World War, I met Sigrid Neset. Sigrid, the only daughter of a Norwegian family, lived in Tregennis Gardens, New Malden, then a recent suburban development to the south-west of London. Until I got a scholarship to the local grammar we attended the same school. Our romance, like most infantile *affaires du coeur*, was intense and because I was three years younger, at times painful, although it hardly progressed beyond the courtly duties of holding hands, performing little favours for the beloved and defending her honour against older predators.

The old poets say that one's first love is never forgotten. They spoke true. The image of this fragile child with her pigtails and her apple-cheeked, blonde Nordic beauty never faded from my mind. Sigrid Neset remained beyond compare; innocent and faultless. My immature promises of devotion unto death were seriously meant – I dared to hope that they were reciprocated.

When the bombing started, London schools were evacuated and I spent the years of conflict in North Wales. For a few months in 1940 I exchanged letters with Sigrid, whose father now worked for the BBC's Foreign Language Service, but for some reason she stopped writing. She had left school and taken a typing job in Wimbledon. Her last letter to me was typed and like the others addressed to "Artie". She had always called me that, although she knew I didn't like it.

On Christmas Eve 1940 most of Tregennis Gardens was reduced to rubble by a land mine. I heard from my mother that all three Nesets were believed to be among the victims of the raid though the bodies of the fifty dead were completely unrecognisable and what was left had been buried in a mass grave.

At first I could not think of my beautiful Sigrid as no longer among the living and for weeks I mourned but at that tender age resilience is strong even to the worst of tragedies and her wraith faded and merged with the diminishing past of childhood. Though I never forgot her completely, other, more masculine loves like competitive games and the Cadet Corps, kept me going throughout a miserable adolescence. In those days the opposite sex did not rank high in the concerns of sixth-formers working against time to pass outstanding examinations before conscription changed their lives.

Just after the war's end I landed in the Army, where my short-sightedness was not considered a serious problem. In the summer of 1946 I was posted to Catterick Camp in Yorkshire for Signals training and in the last week of the course our cadre was invited to a tea-dance in the local Town Hall. I was no dancer and sat down to await delivery of the tea and cakes. After a few minutes of torpor I became conscious of a slim girl in a white dress sitting on the other side of the room. She was staring intently in my direction across the floor with wide-open blue eyes as if she knew me. My natural attraction to her Nordic type overcame my shyness and I screwed up enough courage to request a dance. Imagine my feelings when this vision from my occasional dreams, after one clumsy turn around the floor, asked "You're Artie Knight, aren't you? Remember me, Sigrid Neset? We went to school together when I lived in Tregennis Gardens. We were bombed out".

Halted in my tracks I had to sit down. It is a shock to meet a person alive whom you thought was dead, particularly one who had been so close. In a moment my half-forgotten emotions returned, diluted by time and experience but still identifiable. My first love at second sight? I was utterly overwhelmed by her living presence. Her physical appearance had hardly altered and she still had those pigtails and the fresh complexion of a sixteen-year-old, exactly as I'd known her in London.

She was amused. She had not been in the house when the bomb fell but had luckily left the London area for a Christmas holiday with relatives in Yorkshire. She had been living there ever since and now worked in a Rotherham office. I noticed that she now had a slight local accent. She never mentioned the loss of her parents.

Did we take up where we had left off? Not exactly. Fate in the shape of the Army decreed otherwise. That tea-dance was our last social event before the cadre decamped for the next stage of training and we had only a short time to reminisce and fill the gaps. I did most of the talking. We exchanged addresses, hers a boarding house, mine to be a barracks in Aldershot. I promised to write and I did, twice, but both letters came back weeks later marked "Returned to sender, addressee unknown".

Thus was my romance with Sigrid nipped in the bud for the second time. After passing out from Mons Barracks, I was posted to a Communications Unit in the British Zone of Germany.

That brief encounter would have been my last contact with her had it not been for a letter from my mother, telling of a marriage between Miss Sigrid Neset and a Sergeant George Wilberforce. "Isn't that the little girl you knew at school?" she asked. "The good-looking one? We were all sure she had died in that air-raid. I always thought she'd be a film-star."

I remembered Wilberforce from Catterick. Pending demobilization, he had worked in the camp pharmacy. In his middle thirties, he had been a prisoner of the Japanese and suffered from periodic fits of depression. A bit old for her I thought. I was a bit annoyed that she had never given me any hint of his existence. That no doubt explained the returned letters, if not her broken promise to write. I consoled myself by resorting to a universal truism about the frailty of woman jolly well put by old Shakespeare.

Hence I resolved to blot the elusive Sigrid entirely from my mind, with less regret this time, and while still in the Army took the plunge into matrimony with a German widow five years older than I was but this hastily-conceived arrangement didn't survive in the reduced economic circumstances of civilian life as a grant-aided law student. Trudy was a blonde Rhinemaiden who claimed aristocratic lineage and didn't care for the dull domesticity of South London digs after the lavish entertainments open to occupation troops in Hanover. She left me for a property millionaire.

In 1956, equipped with an undistinguished legal qualification, I scouted round for a congenial job, eventually settling for a place with a firm of family solicitors in the centre of Brighton and renting a comfortable flat within bus range of the office. For a year I led a totally drab life.

That's when I started to advertise in the 'lonely-hearts' columns. You know the kind of thing. 'Ex-officer, 29, divorced, experienced legal professional, many lively interests, wishes to meet Scandinavian-type lady for mutual satisfaction'. I didn't have any lively interests but the rest was nearly true and within days one such 'ad' brought in a score of replies sent to my box number and forwarded.

Of all these petitions only one jerked me into a flurry of excitement. Postmarked Lewes, Sussex, it stated simply that the writer wished to meet me and hoped that her appearance would satisfy my requirements, see enclosed snapshot. Would I care to meet her at noon the following Saturday in the lounge of the Orchard Arms on the cliff-top at Rottingdean?

The letter was typed and signed "Sigrid Wilberforce *née* Neset" and dated June 1st. Delivery must have been delayed as the date was now June 15th. The snapshot, a faded "Polyfoto" in a style popular during the war, made her look very young, little different from the Sigrid I had once worshipped. She even had her pigtails. She had obviously used an old photo. What had become of old George Wilberforce? Had their marriage come adrift? If so, I might be in with a chance, so to speak. Not very noble sentiments, really.

I swiftly replied to her Box Number, identified myself, blamed my delay in responding on the Post Office, supplied my home address and telephone number and agreed to her arrangement for a meeting at what was a convenient rendezvous for both of us. I decided not to ask her back to my flat on this first occasion but to play safe and await developments. She would get a huge surprise when she found out that her old flame "Artie" still yearned to re-enter her life. A strong sense of destiny being fulfilled buoyed up my confidence.

Although no telephone call came to further our relationship in advance of the appointment it never occurred to me that she might not turn up. On the Saturday, Midsummer's Day as it happened, it was very hot, the hottest day of the year so far, with a temperature in the eighties. I got to the Orchard Arms exactly on the stroke of noon and took up a position from which I could watch the door. I waited and waited, fortified by several double gins, my eager pleasure at the prospect of reunion gradually evaporating.

At one o'clock, I was forced to the gloomy conclusion that my Sigrid was, after all, not to be relied upon. Once again she had faded away without a word of explanation. I was weighed down by a deep sense of frustration, alternating with bursts of optimism. Perhaps my letter had gone astray? Could she have mistaken the meeting-place and gone directly to my home address? Hope springs eternal. I caught the one-thirty bus for home and headed somewhat unsteadily for the security of my flat, passing, as usual, the crematorium. A sprinkling of visitors, including an overweight priest, were just going in. Saturday afternoons were popular times for visiting.

It was then that my attention focussed on the far more enticing sight of a slim blonde girl in a white dress walking up the street towards me. I had become even more short-sighted from poring over all those law-books and her features were blurred. My heart thumped. Could it possibly be Sigrid, who, having missed the appointment, was now coming to visit me at home? No, it couldn't, as this one was obviously very young, in her teens, though rather like Sigrid as she had been at that age.

As she came closer, I screwed up my eyes to get a clearer view of her features but she crossed over and abruptly turned into the crematorium gates. Perhaps it was the alcohol, the heat, I don't know why. I wasn't given to stalking young girls, even those who looked as if they might have been doubles of my lifelong ideal of feminine pulchritude, but on this occasion decided I had a defensible excuse so I crossed over and followed her.

The gates were left open daily so that visitors might enter the chapel and linger at the very last earthly destination of their departed loved ones, or the rose garden where the ashes of the deceased were scattered among the flowers. The book of remembrance, a feature of every crematorium chapel, is normally left open at the page marking the date of the death and altered daily.

I'd never been in the place before but noticed that the vista appeared less dismal than that of the average churchyard – no neglected gravestones, leaning monuments overgrown with lichen, Victorian effigies of the dear departed, nor other depressing *memento mori*, apart from rows of plaques let into the red brick wall of the crematorium building itself and inscribed with the names of those whose ashes had not been scattered or removed. Their urns were stored within. It occurred to me that even if corpses might decide to rise from their graves and go walkabout in a churchyard, it wasn't likely to happen in a crematorium!

A gardener kept the paths and lawns trim and maintained the *fauna* and *flora* to a creditable standard so that the natural scene did not offend the casual eye. No-one of my acquaintance had ever been received there and the process of dissolution remained a burning mystery which at the age of twenty-nine I was in no hurry to investigate. I passed the gates every morning on my way to the bus-stop and back in the evenings without giving even a fleeting thought to such arcane matters.

It took me no more than ten seconds to cross the road yet when I strained my eyes beyond the gates along the path I caught a glimpse of a white dress fluttering on the steps leading up to the modern Chapel of Remembrance in the crematorium building, fully fifty yards distant. How had she managed to get there so quickly? I followed, my curiosity aroused; although I knew that this girl couldn't possibly be Sigrid, I just had to have a closer look at her face.

I broke into a run, climbed the steps and opened the door to the chapel. Compared with the heat outside, the temperature was agreeably cool. The rows of pews were empty but some people were inspecting the book of remembrance, today's page open at the list of hand-written entries to remind mourners of those dear departed who had passed through the double doors behind the altar. One of the group was the fat priest. The girl was not to be seen. I had a spooky feeling about this. Where on earth had she gone? At the other end of the Chapel I spotted a green-painted door. After some hesitation, induced by uncertainty, I opened it, expecting to find myself outside again, but there was a steep flight of metal stairs leading to a basement from which the sound of a radio drifted upwards. I descended the stairs calling out "Anybody at home?

There was. A toothy man with a big moustache dressed in grubby overalls and smoking a pipe looked up from his paper. A bottle of beer stood on a deal table. The chief feature of the room was a row of ovens, heavy doors closed. So this was the actual crematorium, the place of incineration. Although the ovens were inactive, their dying heat still hung in the stifling air. I had ventured into the underworld. Apologising for disturbing him I asked if a girl-friend of mine had come down within the last couple of minutes. He showed his teeth.

"Girlfriend? No girls ever come down here … not live ones, anyway," he said, with a rather sinister laugh.

I wanted to escape from this fetid atmosphere and pursue my quest, but he struck up a conversation. His name was Christofi, a Greek Cypriot who kept a weekend eye on the chapel.

"Care to look around?" he asked me.

I didn't, but was unwilling to admit it. Needing no further encouragement he eagerly expounded the mechanics of the cremation process, from the rollers which transported the coffins from the altar through the curtained doors to the fiery furnace which consumed them and their occupants at two thousand degrees Fahrenheit.

"Better than burial," he assured me. "Stops folk coming back after they're dead."

That cogent phrase was to stick in my memory. Warming to his theme, he pointed out the multiple gas-jets which could convert a twelve-stone male corpse into three pounds of white powder in under four hours.

"Women have more fat, go quicker," he added, recalling the Gravedigger in *Hamlet* – another mine of information on bodily disintegration. I hadn't thought it took that long, as the human body is eighty plus percent water, but apparently the bones were resistant to the flames and had to be ground down small with a mortar and pestle before they could be collected in the casket. Only the quick-burning cedar-wood coffins were reduced to ashes. The human remains were carefully separated. He ridiculed the popular myth of black smoke pouring out of the chimney. People would complain.

Mr Christofi's expert discourse had blunted the original purpose of my intrusion into his domain. He was a gruesome-minded fellow. It was high time to seek a polite retreat, so I bade him farewell and ascended the steps into the clear air with relief. Not much point in looking for the girl now, I thought. The mid-afternoon heat was overpowering and the long-term effects of those double gins had reduced my enthusiasm for further action but, contrary to my expectations, there she was. I could just make out the flash of her white dress among the rose bushes inside the Garden of Remembrance. She must have gone through the chapel and straight out by some other exit which I hadn't noticed.

Somehow I had to get close enough to her to make sure, but what should I do then? Introduce myself? I quickened my pace and followed my barely visible quarry into the garden, but then, inexplicably, I lost her. In a trice, she had vanished. The rose bushes and cypresses in the garden were fenced off to a height of five feet and there was no way by which a living person could have got out without jumping the fence or emerging by the gate. I explored the whole area, about an acre of ground, without result.

Puzzled and apprehensive, I was ready to cut my losses and go home when I noticed that a scattering ceremony was in progress. Close to the access-gate the same priest whom I'd seen twice before was reading from a prayer book and supporting a thin man in conventional black mourning-clothes who was in a very distraught state. A balding man and a woman wearing a purple headscarf, both elderly, stood in attendance with heads bowed.

The priest intoned a prayer and the thin man, who looked terrified out of his wits, shook a polished wooden casket until it had shed its contents. A fine whitish shower faintly visible against the sky was carried off by a sudden wind as the priest recited what I at first took to be the standard committal service in English but when he continued chanting angrily in Latin and punctuated his words with violent gestures I decided that I was watching an exorcism.

This strange scene had attracted a curious crowd and I heard the woman with the headscarf explain that they'd "burnt a witch and she's gone for ever!" Her companion announced that this was done to make sure that the doomed soul was purified and that she didn't come back to earth full-bodied. I remembered the wisdom of Mr Christofi.

The priest ended his incantations and abruptly strode off, leaving the other three gathered under a cypress tree. Something about the distraught man struck me as familiar and when I saw his heavily-lined face doubts as to his identity vanished. He was George Wilberforce, Sigrid's husband, looking about sixty, and here was I, Arthur Knight, trying to embark on an *affaire* with his wife. Any prick of conscience on my part was brief, however. After all, she had made the running. Wilberforce wouldn't remember an anonymous soldier from all those years ago and I certainly had no desire to reveal myself to him. I made myself scarce.

As I started up the stairs to my flat on the second floor my telephone was ringing. Not many people had the number and the law office was closed at weekends. Could it be Sigrid? I fairly hurled myself across the narrow hallway, dropping my doorkey in the process, desperate to get at that urgently shrilling instrument.

Hoping against hope I managed to blurt out the words, "Sigrid, is that you?"

At first I was greeted by complete silence and nervously demanded to know who was calling. Then came a series of clanking noises, what sounded like the slamming of a door and the most horrible agonised wail that I'd ever heard. Finally a muffled voice, very weak, whispered two words in my ear. I thought it said "sorry Artie" or perhaps "see you, Artie" before an eerie whistling and a rush of static was succeeded by a hollow silence.

I tried to call the exchange to see if they could tell me where the call had come from but the line was dead. I remembered with a start that my office had actually reported it out of order two days before. Ever since that ghastly afternoon I've wondered what I'd really heard in this moment of high tension. Only one person had ever called me "Artie".

There followed a sleepless night of bad dreams in which I stumbled through a wood trying with leaden feet to catch up with the girl in white but she eluded me and turned into the fat priest who showed me the page of a book but as is common in dreams, I couldn't make out the words. I got a funny feeling about that, especially when the identical dream – or nightmare rather – persisted throughout the week.

One obvious way to banish such uneasy visions is to face up to the underlying reality, so I went back to the chapel, hoping that the Book of Remembrance was kept bang up-to-date covering the current week. It wasn't, but as it happened that didn't matter. The most recent entry, in black print, had been made on an otherwise blank page weeks earlier, dated June 1st, and read:

"In Loving Memory of Sigrid Neset, a Witch aged Sixteen Years, Gone to her Eternal Rest. From her Beloved Husband".

I noted the age, and the date, at first with quickening incredulity, then with a void in the pit of my stomach and a gnawing sense of having suffered a species of deprivation far beyond my understanding. Eternal Rest? What bereaved husband would omit his wife's married surname and reduce her age by half let alone enter such a (literally) damning inscription in a book of remembrance and even if he wanted to perpetuate her memory in such an outlandish fashion no orthodox Christian chapel would tolerate such a legacy. There was something peculiar here.

Sigrid a witch? Yes, in a sense she was. She had certainly bewitched me and, as it turned out, many others too. This was revealed when Wilberforce, described as a 'pharmacist, aged 47' was tried at Lewes Assizes for her murder. But the capital charge failed for lack of material evidence, to wit, the body, destroyed, the prosecution alleged, by an illegal cremation; an "inside job" for which my subterranean acquaintance Christofi was arraigned as an accomplice. That corpulent priest and the participants in the "exorcism", all three relatives of the accused Wilberforce, called in to give evidence, claimed that the ashes they had scattered were those of a cat.

Wilberforce insisted that his wife was alive and had left him for another man – one of many whom she had met through a contact magazine. Much was made of his experiences as a prisoner of the Japanese and the well-substantiated perfidy of his wife. The jury was sympathetic and gave him the benefit of the doubt. Both he and Christofi were found not guilty but recalled to face minor charges. The entry in the book was not mentioned, which I thought odd, as it seemed to provide evidence of some sort. My name never came into it and I reckoned I'd been lucky. The firm wouldn't have appreciated the publicity.

After the trial I returned to the chapel to look at the book again. Though I scrutinized every page for the previous year, the entry for June 1st was simply not to be found, nor had the volume been mutilated in any way.

Although my rental contract still had a few months to run, I left the flat for a bedsit in Shoreham, miles away from that crematorium. I don't believe in witches but I set no store in exorcisms either.

Some may say that the foregoing narrative bears more than a passing resemblance to the ancient Greek legend of Orpheus and Eurydice, though Orpheus lost his beloved Eurydice to the shades twice only and in one late version of the tale actually got her back for good. I don't think I deserve that.

2. Hand's Tale

I heard the following story when I was working as a tour guide for a cruise line. My account of what the eccentric Mr Hand claimed had happened to him on this particular tropical island tries to stay faithful to his own version, but as I got it second-hand (no pun intended) from a regular cruising couple named Sorley who had been on the spot, something may have been lost in the retelling.

The year before he died, Edgar Hand, aged 62 and single, treated himself – on retirement from preparatory school teaching – to a Caribbean cruise. It was his first, inspired by late middle-aged notions of "meeting someone", but as the *Sea Oyster* wound from island to island his hopes gradually receded and he contented himself with shipboard social activities and forays ashore by local taxi.

Early one afternoon, towards the end of the cruise, the ship dropped anchor on Bellucine Island in the Bahamas for a six-hour stay and those passengers wishing to explore what was to most of them unfamiliar territory were carried to the shore by tender. A warning against the strong undertow was issued to discourage people from venturing too far from the beach. Hand, uncomfortable even in the chlorinated water at the shallow end of swimming-pools, had no intention of venturing into unpredictable salty depths.

The Berry chain of islands lies fifty miles from Florida, divided into North and South Bimini and numerous cays or small islands, of which Bellucine, similarly separated into North and South, had recently started to attract tourists in spite of or perhaps because of its reputation as an off-shore retreat for gangsters from the mainland. *Sea Oyster* dropped anchor half a mile from the quayside where local taxi-drivers, who relied on passing cruise-ships for a precarious seasonal income, lined up in the hope of talking short-time visitors from the tenders into splashing out on a guided trip.

Hand was one of the last to step on the uneven jetty which divided the narrow ribbon of sand leading to the tar-macadamed road and a native village of dilapidated shacks. He was dismayed to find that the regular taxis had already found customers and were disappearing into the distance.

That is, all bar one, a solitary vehicle, a battered Ford Mercury, dating from the early fifties and parked some distance from the landing stage, remained as yet uncharted. A small, bespectacled negro with a goatee beard and wearing a rusty black suit with a high collar barely hiding a livid weal which encircled his neck, saluted the Englishman and in a pseudo-American argot, introduced himself as Joseph and launched into his 'spiel'.

"How're you Sir? Care for a trip? Two hours and I'll show you everythin' … includin' places the other guys won't go. Sixty dollars US. No extras, no kidding. How about it sir? You won't regret it…"

Hand hesitated. Sixty dollars sounded fair by shore-excursion standards and if he wanted to see the island within the time-limit, this was clearly the best way to do it. Where could this fellow go on such a small island that the others wouldn't, he wondered, and why wouldn't they?

Curiosity decided for him. Hoping that the man was trustworthy, he surrendered to Joseph, who ushered him into the rear of the old Ford and deftly steered it through the tourists fingering the trinkets displayed on the ramshackle stalls and away from the colourful bustle of the quayside. The smooth tar-macadam ran out on the other side of the village, leaving the vehicle to bump wearily over potholes at about fifteen miles per hour. Hand soon realised that the twin islands, connected by a narrow causeway, were together no more than a dozen miles long and that even at this leisurely speed, two hours would be ample for the tour. The notable attraction for regular visitors to the area was offshore and lay mainly in big-game fishing for sailfish. The capital, Barke Town, with its bars and nightclubs, provided recreation in the evenings. The greater part of the population of twelve hundred lived on the North Island; in the fifties the ubiquitous Ernest Hemingway had been one of them.

Joseph reeled off these and other well-rehearsed statistics as they rattled along the dirt road within a few yards of the beach. The potholed route was marked by a number of churches, some with extravagant baroque architecture. The Holy Name Catholic church stood out in the shape of an Egyptian pyramid. The larger houses spoke only of neglect.

Hand knew that the island might have served as an ideal recreation spot for genuine long-term visitors from Florida – had not local corruption and the attentions of an offshore Mafia ever-ready to employ violence ruined its prospects. The old familiar sad story of post-colonial lost opportunity, he decided. A brief halt at yet another dilapidated mansion, windows broken and its concrete patio overgrown by weeds and another longer stop by an abandoned factory confirmed the general impression of what might have been.

Joseph retraced his route across the causeway for about a mile and headed along a parallel and deeply-rutted side-track edged on both sides by palm trees through which an occasional glimpse of blue-green waters beyond provided the only relief from the gloom.

All at once Hand made up his mind that he had already seen enough of this exhausted place. More than that, he felt a tinge of apprehension. Did all the local taxis bring their tourist clients here? He hadn't passed a single one since starting out. He looked at his watch – a full hour still to go – time to get back to the ship, he decided.

Joseph must have read his thoughts as he resumed the running commentary.

"Plenty of time yet sir. Interestin' history in these parts. Did you know that Bimini was once the lost island of Atlantis that sank beneath the sea and came up again? And the Fountain of Youth – drink the waters and you'll live forever – but no-one's sure exactly where to find it, though people have been looking for five centuries, ever since Ponçe de Leon in the sixteenth century. A few interestin' items on Bellucine as well. For instance, we had a leper colony here. Care to look at where they were buried? Not many have seen it. You enjoy good health sir?"

His passenger shrugged. "It's all right", he answered, unwilling to go into details of respiratory ailments contracted on board the *Sea Oyster*, but Joseph did not wait for an answer and braked sharply.

"You're a lucky man, sir, and now we'll stop for a minute and you can see the scariest spot on this island. You look as though you don't frighten easily sir."

Had the fellow not offered this back-handed compliment Hand would have ordered him directly to drive on back to the quayside, but with his bravery put to the test, he felt he had no option but to conceal his annoyance. Might as well take what was on offer, he said to himself as Joseph pulled up by a thick clump of bush and motioned him to disembark, lighting a cheroot and pointing at some rough steps leading to a stony path half-hidden by vegetation.

"Down there you'll see an old burial-place, most of them lepers who died a long while ago", Joseph explained with a wide-
mouthed grin. "Nobody comes here, not even in the daylight –
not many tourists have your nerve sir. People are scared of meeting someone they'd be wiser not to meet... but I reckon you're
not one of those. Go on down."

"Aren't you coming?" queried Hand, but Joseph shook his
head, drew on his cheroot, expelled a wreath of smoke, grinned
again, closed his eyes and lolled back on the seat.

Not wishing to appear nervous, Hand resolved to look for
himself, resenting the man's implication that an Englishman
might lack the courage to penetrate the obscurity of this inhospitable hollow. Very little sunlight filtered through the ring of palm
trees which encircled the dreary place and hid it from the road
above.

Descending the crude steps, he came upon a clear patch on
the sharply sloping ground running down to a rocky section of
the seashore. The surrounding coconut palms had grown densely
for many years and kept the direct heat away, leaving the air
stifling and fetid. Close to the beach a number of grave-markers
stuck up at odd angles. Gingerly, he climbed down until he was
standing on a level with the stones and started to walk around
them, trying to read the inscriptions, but most of them had been
eroded by time and weather and Hand could discern only fragments of names and dates. Not much of a tourist attraction.

"Be up in a minute!" he called, but Joseph did not answer. The
dense growth blocked any sound from outside and only the faint
wash of the breakers below penetrated the dead silence.

It was then that he noticed a lone swimmer coming towards
the shore at a fast crawl but still a fair distance out. Hand could
just make out the pale blob of a face and the agitation as the
swimmer rapidly approached. That fellow must be really at home

in the water, he thought, but another wave of unease urged him to quit this spooky hole and return to the taxi. Why hadn't Joseph come down with him? Surely it was a guide's job to stay with his charges?

"Hey you there... Joseph?" he shouted, but realised there was no need to call out, for there was Joseph himself standing right behind him. Odd that he hadn't heard the fellow descending.

"Oh, here you are. I thought..."

The sentence died in his throat, for the newcomer was not Joseph but an older negro in an ancient dark suit, wearing a wide-brimmed straw hat with a dirty whitish cloth wrapped around his head which partly covered his features. Hand did not feel inclined to look too closely at them and though he sought to combat his sudden alarm by muttering a greeting, the other did not reply and appeared to be concentrating on something far out to sea.

Hand decided it must be the swimmer, who was now much closer to the shore and heading directly for the ground where they both were standing. It occurred to him that the latter might be yet another personage whom – in Joseph's remembered words – it was wiser not to meet. Best to climb back up to the road.

"I'm on my way..." he called. His words echoed around the circle of trees and sounded oddly distorted, as though they were being strained through cotton wool.

But now came horrors anew. The first visitant was silently joined by others of like appearance, at least a dozen of them, looming by the now-open graves, blurred shapes of men and women clad in ill-fitting garments, each with those grubby lengths of pale linen cloth wound about their heads. Hand gave out a strangled scream. Lepers! Images from uncanny tales were turning into reality.

The tattered apparitions crowded in on him as he scrambled up the slope, slipping awkwardly on the rough steps in his haste. He fancied that they were clutching at him as in a child's nightmare of pursuit, though this was surely no dream. The thought of their ghastly touch appalled him. Contact, he was sure, must mean leprous contagion and death, but the bodies did not seem to be solidly physical and in a moment of strange calm Hand fancied that he could see through them to the graves from which they must have emerged.

A pervasive earthy smell flooded into Hand's nostrils and he retched violently. He could think only that he had dropped into another dimension. His terror drove him to desperate action and he made a violent effort to force his leaden feet up the rough steps. Stark thoughts of contamination paralysed his reason, leaving him stripped of all instincts save that of self-preservation and the basic human urge to get back to a familiar world.

Sweating with fear, he dragged his body up through the bush and blindly staggered out at the top of the slope near where he had left the taxi.

Alas, any hope of quick release faded in a flash. The old Ford and the voluble Joseph were no longer there. Along with his fear, he felt anger at the man's desertion. Had it been deliberate – a plan to betray him to the hungry ghouls, zombies, *revenants* or whatever they were?

The narrow stretch of dusty road was deserted as far as he could see until it faded round a bend about fifty yards distant. The bright light had given place to a blanket of dark thundery cloud cutting off the sun, promising one of those short, drenching tropical downpours, regular afternoon features of the island weather. As the first drops of heavy rain descended he was glad to see on the curve of the road the welcome sight of a car coming towards him. His first reaction was one of relief. It just had to be

Joseph returning to pick him up and he hailed the vehicle. He felt a return of anger at the fellow and at himself for his wild idea that the elusive driver was an ally of the dead, perhaps walking dead himself, an exile from Haiti.

He waved. It was not the unreliable Joseph's taxi but an almost new Mercedes, which pulled up immediately. Hand laughed aloud at his own loss of nerve. This taxi, with a uniformed driver, was carrying a couple of elderly passengers named Sorley, who happened to share his dinner-table.

"Going back to the ship?" he asked breathlessly, trying to look normal. "My taxi-man seems to have deserted me."

"Be our guest," said Mr Sorley. "You look as if you've seen a ghost."

'In the plural,' thought Hand, and scrambled in, crouching in the front seat as they gathered speed. He experienced a momentary feeling of relief, but a glimpse of activity on the road ahead revived the clutching terror.

Running out from the roadside was a young man in his early twenties, whose bronzed body glistened and dripped with sea-water. He was not alone. Coming up from the depths of the bush behind him were several dark shapes with their heads wrapped in whitish linen cloths.

The swimmer, features frozen in terror, lurched directly into the path of the car, holding up his hand palm outwards.

Hand heard his own strangled voice calling to the driver to stop and then frantically, "Watch out! You'll hit him!"

Far from slowing down, the Mercedes driver accelerated and drove ahead as though no-one barred his path. There was no discernible impact and Hand thought that the swimmer must have jumped aside at the last moment.

He had a momentary sighting of a frightened face with red-dish hair and European features. Turning to look back through the rear window to find out what had happened he saw an empty road; the young man and his grisly pursuers had vanished.

Hand looked wildly at the Sorleys. Mr Sorley was beginning to regret having picked him up.

"The young man's been hurt. Why didn't this fool stop! The poor chap must have been thrown into the ditch."

"Young man? What young man was that?" asked Mr Sorley. "I didn't see anybody." He ordered his driver to pull up but the fellow shook his head and increased speed.

Mr Sorley shrugged. "He doesn't seem too keen on the idea, and frankly I'm not surprised. Whatever it was you think you saw, old chap, it's not there now. Trick of the light."

Hand was speechless. This rapid succession of disconnected and inexplicable events, moved by some weird force that had chosen him as spectator, inhibited his desire to explain what had happened and he sat out the rest of the journey dumbly recovering. Mrs Sorley, a managing sort of woman, was more concerned than her husband on Hand's account. She was most indignant when she learned that his first taxi had left him in the lurch. Hand reluctantly agreed to lodge a complaint against Joseph, though he did not think it would do much good.

Back at the quayside, Mrs Sorley's efforts on behalf of her dazed passenger turned up a well-spoken Bahamian in a blazer who introduced himself in an exaggerated "Oxford" accent as Mr Arlington-Thomas and claimed official responsibility for the conduct of local taxis. He was accompanied by a sad-looking woman in a flowered frock whom he said, with an intrusive grin, was his "chief assistant".

Affecting incredulity he assured the visitors that none of his drivers would neglect passengers or lead them astray to be set upon by robbers. The firm he represented had got to give the cruise lines satisfactory service and to show good will he offered to return the sixty dollars. Hand declined, explaining that Joseph hadn't actually taken the fare.

Joseph? Mr Arlington-Thomas shook his head. Of course, he knew all the drivers. A common enough name, but nobody called Joseph worked for him. An old Ford Mercury? Impossible sir. Registration here is very strict. None of our taxis are more than a couple of years old. Could have been an unlicensed car, in which case it is a matter for the police. Did this Joseph have a uniform? All our employees wear uniforms.

The female assistant looked pensive and muttered something about a taxi-man who had murdered a tourist. Mr Arlington-Thomas dismissed this clearly unwelcome interruption which he said referred to an incident "a long time ago" and in any case happened in Bimini.

Reluctantly Hand did his best to describe the graveyard and the strange denizens he had found there. Lepers? Mr Arlington-Thomas's disbelief was barely concealed. He insisted that they must have been petty thieves, preying on visitors, though he'd never heard of any recent trouble of that sort on any of the islands. Old burials? From the leper colony? Yes, there had been a graveyard. He knew where it used to be but it was bulldozed many years ago by the American gentleman who owned the land at that time, a Mr Earl Drury. Come to think of it, his son Red had been found dead on the road just off that same beach. He had been an Olympic swimmer. They said he'd had a heart attack in the water but word got around that he'd been deliberately run down by a car. Mr Earl Drury went back to America. Most likely it was something to do with the gangs out of Miami. Bad criminals. Mr Arlington-Thomas straightened his striped tie and sighed. "Some of the locals here are very superstitious and believe in duppies ... you know ... ghosts of dead folk. Plenty of stories in the islands about haunted places. No graveyard there now sir.

Would you care to drive back in one of our cars free of charge and check it out?"

On an impulse Hand asked if the son had been called "Red" because of the colour of his hair. Mr Arlington-Thomas had never met the young man but thought it was a common American nickname and quite possible. Hand had no desire to take up Mr Arlington-Thomas's offer to "check it out" and the "robbers" explanation did not convince.

He resolved not to elaborate further at this stage on his brief encounter with the swimmer and the "accident" which only he had claimed to have witnessed. It was plain that his hearers, including the Sorleys, thought him still in shock. Besides, he sure, in the safety of present company, that he hadn't been a victim of hallucinations and that the only reality had been the unexplained desertion of Joseph. Although the Sorleys and an embarrassed Mr Arlington-Thomas accompanied him on an inspection of the returning taxis and the area round the village in the faint hope of encountering the fellow but no-one resembling the errant driver nor any old Ford Mercury plying for hire was to be seen.

He was walking back to the tender alone when a soft female voice broke into his concentration. It belonged to Mr Arlington-Thomas's downtrodden assistant, who introduced herself shyly as Mrs Arlington-Thomas and apologised for what had happened to him on the island. Whatever her husband might say, she believed in the story about Joseph. It was true that a man who drove a taxi had once joined up with a gang who waylaid tourists but "your" Joseph couldn't have been the same. That particular scoundrel had been taken to Nassau and hanged, years ago. There must be another wicked rascal calling himself Joseph. She would tell her husband to inform the police.

Hand opened his mouth to acquaint Mrs Arlington-Thomas with what he remembered about "his" Joseph's neck, but thought better of it. Her explanation was more comfortable.

Mentally drained, he boarded the waiting tender for return to the *Sea Oyster*, supported by the sympathetic Mrs Sorley and seen off by a relieved Mr Arlington-Thomas. The cruise ship sailed at six to the accompaniment of her resident five-piece band and the jetty, the quayside buildings, the natives loafing outside the shacks and the section of tarmac road where he had started on his memorable island tour soon merged and became indistinct.

As the vessel drew out into the open sea and Bellucine receded into the sunset, Hand, leaning over the rail, waved a relieved farewell to the lush panorama, with its swaying palm trees, yellow beaches, white sails of yachts and silhouettes of fishing-boats riding the turquoise waters. He vowed that no inducement would ever persuade him to return.

At dinner a few days later he confided the full story of his experience to the Sorleys, who passed it on to me. Mr Sorley thought it mainly fiction but Mrs Sorley didn't believe the man had been making it up simply to impress an audience on a table for six. I thought they were judging him rather harshly, although he did include one item which his hearers decided was an embellishment that might well have been left out. He told them that when the ship was about a mile distant from the quayside his eye had caught the strenuous action of a man swimming rapidly towards the beach but when he found the spot with his binoculars a couple of seconds later the sea was clear.

Hearing this, Mr Sorley had dryly asked him if the chap by any chance had red hair, whereupon Hand, apparently much offended, left the table and retired to his cabin.

3. *The Spirit of the Loch*

In the spring of 1943, Flight-Sergeant Bourne, aged twenty-six and navigator with a Beaufighter squadron based in Lossiemouth happened on a muddy painting in a *bric-à-brac* shop in Elgin, a cheerless daub, unsigned and showing an old castle with three indistinct figures looking out from a misty headland over uniformly grey waters. The artist had given his uninspired work a title, *The Spirit of the Loch,* and Bourne reckoned that only the frame made it worth the asking price of five shillings.

He presented it to the NCOs Mess, where it occupied a place above the bar and became a target for darts. Warrant-Officer Lauder, his pilot, was a swarthy twenty-two-year-old Highlander, whose home was, for him, conveniently placed a few miles from the northern extreme of Loch Ness. He immediately recognised the locale of the picture as Urquhart Castle. Its title was close to the inscription he had painted under the cockpit of their aeroplane – *The Spirit of Loch Ness*, after Charles Lindbergh's *Spirit of St Louis*. 'Lindy' had achieved fame as the first man to fly the Atlantic solo and Lauder hoped that he might inherit some of the American's luck and get through the war in one piece.

The third member of the *"Spirit's"* crew was Sergeant Topley, aged twenty, radar operator and in civilian life a professional photographer, naturally keen on adding panoramic views of the famous stretch of water to his collection. Loch Ness inevitably suggested 'monster', but the war had practically killed off public interest in the beast. Nevertheless the remote possibility of capturing that enigmatic creature on film undoubtedly gave Topley an extra incentive.

One Saturday morning Lauder drove his crew from 'Lossie' in his father's Standard 12 and after a pub-lunch in Inverness the trio set out for the loch. Mist patches were starting to develop along the north shore and sombre cloud patches were mirrored in the water. Lauder himself was endowed with much of the mystical nature long associated with Highlanders but Bourne had been brought up in the streets of South London and looked at life unromantically with the blasé attitudes of the urban dweller. Even so, he was scarcely prepared for that first intimidating sight of the blue-grey waters, deepening to black when no sun shone and shielding impenetrable layers of mystery which, it seemed to him, no human being might hope to plumb.

Had Bourne been a student of literature he might have been familiar with an Old English poet able to catch its chill menace – the anonymous author of *Beowulf,* who told of the monster Grendel lurking in the depths of the lonely mere "where well-rooted trees, draped with frost, overshroud the wave with shadowing gloom", but in that ancient bard's mind hovered the awesome spectre of a fiendish enemy of the human race, nothing like the strange "water-kelpie" long associated with the loch nor the familiar 'Nessie' of more recent vintage.

Topley could hardly wait to focus his camera on the view from the Castle, a ruined observer of mediaeval conflict and the finest point-of-vantage over the deepest and widest expanse of the loch. The three men stood on the headland for some time, mesmerized by the continuous swirl of the waters and the spray churning around the hidden rocks. With a start, Bourne remembered how that depressing work of art he'd picked up had placed three people near this identical spot, though the unknown painter had brought out only the obviously gloomy features and completely failed to convey its subtleties. No place to stay for long. Just where one might expect to come across a beast with a long neck rising for a breather, he thought, and shivered. Indeed, Bourne's reverie was interrupted by Topley, who thought he had caught "something shiny, like a fire" in his lens but with the naked eye Bourne saw only a swirl of fog and the uninviting mile-stretch across the loch to the opposite shore.

Their mood was infectious. Most "monster sightings" had originated in the shadow of the castle and generations of journalists had dubbed it 'sinister' – a romantic writer's way of describing a place where persons ready and willing to be deceived might very well mistake some waterborne natural phenomena for a swimming creature with a giraffe neck and humps. Lauder, never much of a talker, stretched out his arm like an Old Testament prophet and announced gravely that "the spirit of the loch is waiting out there for one of us". At that moment Bourne had a strong premonition that he alone of the three would survive the war.

Topley developed the film himself. It included excellent shots of the castle and the widest tract of the water, but nothing resembling a monster appeared on any of his exposures, though close scrutiny of one did reveal an object on the surface about half-a-mile distant that might have been a small boat with a black sail. The trio never returned to the loch shore, but Bourne was beset by a sense of something lurking round the corner, so to speak, waiting to pounce. He mentioned it to Lauder, who said he knew what that must be. There were no more weekend jaunts in his car. Not a good sign, thought Bourne.

The usually cheerful Topley complained of insomnia and the MO threatened to ground him. Bourne wondered if he should apply for a transfer to another crew, but several weeks passed without incident and he decided to let fate take its course. An 'old sweat' who had survived the trenches in 1917 came into the Mess and told Topley an old Arab tale about 'an appointment in

Samarrah' – a rendezvous with Death which could not be avoided. Lauder happened to be within earshot. He apparently knew the story and grabbed the man by the collar. That was the day Bourne noticed that the painting hanging above the bar had gone. No-one seemed to know or care what had happened to it. That was also the day, in the second week of October, when the sudden doom that forever threatened wartime flyers reached out for the crew of "*The Spirit of Loch Ness*".

Airborne from Lossie following a "Red Alert" the Beaufighter had barely gained operational altitude when a wandering *Ju88* intruder from the nearest Luftwaffe base at Stavanger fired a deadly burst of cannon shells from below at close range and "The Spirit", fatally stricken, went straight down out of control with both engines on fire. Bourne thought he heard Lauder's strangled order to bail out and reached for his parachute, only to find it ablaze. Then came the hopeless confusion of those final seconds in the flaming Beaufighter, the searing stench of burning oil, the agonized cries of the others and a loud explosion behind him.

Next he heard a wild rushing of wind accompanied by a weird but not unpleasant sensation of slow gyration. For a moment he felt his body ascending, lifted away from the blazing aircraft. Then the screaming of the shattered engines was gone and only silence remained. Cold air revived him. He found himself erect, waist deep in shallow water and enclosed in a cocoon of total darkness. He felt no pain, only a sensation of release from all that had formerly mattered.

At first Bourne was sure this was death, and not so bad after all, but after a few minutes he grasped the fact that he was still in this world. The ancient story of that appointment in Samarrah floated back, mixed up with the Beaufighter and her last moments. Struggling out of the water he lay semi-conscious for what seemed hours until a Home Guard patrol found him, frozen and wordless but seemingly uninjured, with no sign of burns anywhere on his body. Hot coffee was poured out for him but his rescuers were unfriendly. They seemed to think he must be a German spy. "Whaur's yer parachute than?" was a repeated question. He hardly understood a word in their gruff accents but the atmosphere of suspicion evaporated when the guard commander found his identity-disc and he found himself able to talk. He was loaded into an ambulance and learned that "*The Spirit*", trailing flames, had fallen into the very loch from which she took her name.

"Did you find the others?" he kept asking. But Lauder and Topley were not seen alive again.

After a spell in hospital Bourne was returned to his unit for a few days pending a temporary posting to a navigational instruction unit in Yorkshire. He became aware of an awed silence whenever he came into the Mess at Lossie. Someone had returned that dreary picture to its place above the bar and he noticed that only one figure was now looking out from the headland. Hadn't there been three? He couldn't remember. Before leaving for the south Bourne visited Lauder's father, but the old man seemed wary of him. A letter of sympathy he sent to Topley's parents drew only a formal reply.

Renowned in the service as the airman who bailed out without a 'chute, Flight-sergeant Bourne was grounded for the duration and taught navigation to air cadets until he was demobilized just before his thirtieth birthday in 1946. He qualified as an accountant and got a job with a small firm in a county town. Frequently asked to explain how he'd escaped death, he evolved a romantic formula for dealing with the unanswerable question and said he'd been rescued by "the spirit of the loch", a benevolent force that had saved him. Why him they queried, why not the other two? Was he destined to escape death for no other reason than to solve the financial problems of his firm's clients? For that he had no formula.

In the 1970s came a wave of enthusiasm for raising sunken or buried wartime aircraft – a Wellington bomber that had crashed into the loch in 1944 became the object of an underwater search. The Beau attracted similar attention, not only because of the "monster" connection but also through Bourne, whose 1943 exploit had never been forgotten by writers on aviation. Others had jumped without parachutes rather than burn alive and survived by landing in haystacks or soft snow, but their experiences could all be accounted for by "luck" or divine intervention. Bourne's, in the popular mind touched by the supernatural, had no parallel.

Loch Ness is rumoured to be of "immeasurable" depth, which means in reality about nine hundred feet. For years teams of amateurs and professional "monster-hunters" mounted sophisticated expeditions and courted publicity without delivering evidence of the beast's existence, or non-existence for that matter. It soon became obvious that the chances of raising the Beau intact were about the same as of finding the elusive "Nessie" and the project was soon abandoned. After so many years it was considered that whatever might be left of the machine must be deep in mud.

To bolster publicity for "Nessie" a TV documentary was mounted to mark the fiftieth anniversary of the first sighting. Bourne, retired, unmarried, in his mid-sixties and suffering badly from arthritis, was roped in once again as the miracle survivor and paraded as a secondary attraction to enhance the newly-opened "Loch Ness Monster Exhibition" at Drumnadrochit behind Urquhart Bay, the very place of his mysterious salvation. After the TV crew had departed Bourne was thankfully left to himself. He set out to walk the short road to the Castle and for the first time in forty years stood on the headland looking out over the wind-driven waters to the craggy shore opposite. Overcome by memories, his gaze drifted idly until it was held by a blurred object rising to the surface not more than two hundred yards distant. His eyesight had deteriorated with age but even so he could not be mistaken. At first he took it to be his own close-up "Nessie sighting"? It was certainly an odd shape for a prehistoric monster, black, underslung nacelles, distinctive high rudder, a flash of sunlight on the glazed cockpits and a painted inscription on the bullet nose. He was unable to read the words but knew beyond a shadow of doubt what they must be. In a daze, he let fall his walking-stick as he sensed that two ghostly companions had joined him. Lauder and Topley were there, silent and immobile, in their old flying clothes, heads upturned as if searching the sky. They seemed to glance with faint recognition at this bespectacled elderly man hunched up against the penetrating cold.

Bourne felt no fear of these apparitions. For a third time the loch had touched him with her beneficent spirit, charging him with a series of insoluble riddles, the inspiration of that unknown artist's prophetic scene, the enigma of his unaccountable survival, the unexpected vision of his old warplane, the timeless *revenants* who in life had been his comrades, the calming power of the mysteries binding him to this inhospitable spot.

He understood then that the unfathomable loch had been chosen from time immemorial as a repository of things not to be revealed and would never yield up its secrets. There were no answers, only questions.

Bourne turned to find himself alone and when he again scanned the waters, he could make out only the hazy shape of a fishing-boat.

4. *Winslett's Last Waltz*

When I heard it from his own lips I found Winslett's account hard to swallow except that he was never the sort to invent things. I knew him for more than ten years, a quiet self-contained chap, a retired bank manager whose abounding passion during his working life had been music, particularly the romantic piano repertoire He couldn't play himself but he'd go miles to attend a recital and owned a valuable collection of recordings, many of them rare items, old 78s, LPs and tapes taken off the radio. There weren't many long dead performers he hadn't heard on record if not in the flesh – Rachmaninoff, Hofmann, de Pachmann, Cortot, Gieseking, Solomon, Moiseiwitsch – all the big names of yesteryear. He'd been a 'fan' since the early thirties, when his mother first introduced him to the great masters at the old Queen's Hall.

Winslett's weird experience started one warm July evening on the upper deck of a Number 88 bus somewhere between Streatham and Marble Arch. He picked up a copy of the *Evening Standard* left on a seat and spotted a notice of a Woolgar Hall recital by the American pianist Ilya Dragorin, due to start that very evening in under an hour. His watch told him that it was nearly seven, allowing enough time for him to get there if he missed dinner. He had already missed lunch but Dragorin's was a big name, a world-famous exponent of romantic music whose dazzling recording of the Third Rachmaninoff Concerto was a prize item in Winslett's extensive collection. Given the option of eating or of hearing such a distinguished artist in person Winslett had no doubt as to his preference. Something about the famous musician had been in the news recently but whatever it was eluded his memory.

Passing Hyde Park Corner he felt slightly dizzy but put it down to having skipped lunch. He was a bachelor and inclined to neglect himself. He had never suffered from vertigo before and was relieved when the bus reached Marble Arch, fairly close to his destination. At that time of year it was broad daylight and Oxford Street was crowded with late shoppers. Winslett took care to walk slowly and got to Wigmore Street at twenty to eight, five minutes early. Would he be able to get a ticket? His dizzy spell had passed, to be replaced by the crushing beginnings of a migraine headache.

At the door of the concert-hall he found little sign of activity. The usual queue was absent. Surely the grand name of Ilya Dragorin might be expected to attract a sizeable audience of *aficionados*? There was no poster announcing the programme. Later he was to recall that precise time, 7.41, as the moment of his detachment from the world at large, denoted by an abrupt muffling of familiar street noises and distortion of voices, shifting pedestrians and traffic uncomfortably out-of-focus.

Winslett's migraine attack was affecting his eyesight, narrowing his field of vision and surrounding objects within it with a bright golden veil. Most men would have lost their concentration completely and gone home, but Winslett was not one to abandon such an opportunity on account of a *malaise* which he was sure would wear off in a few minutes.

Consulting his watch, he looked in vain for an informative billboard outside and concluded not without a degree of relief that the performance had been cancelled at the last minute. These things happened, particularly with famous artists. Michelangeli, another outstanding interpreter of the nineteenth century masters, was notorious for his last-minute disappointments. Winslett closed his eyes and leaned against the wall, almost ready to yield to an overwhelming desire to leave when a soft American voice whispered in his ear "Here, sir, you take this ticket, I can't use it".

He swivelled his aching head to see who his transatlantic bene-factor might be but could not bring his eyes to bear on the owner of the voice, who faded into the anonymity of the street. Winslett would normally have speculated on the source of this unexpected good fortune but his odd state of mind urged him to concentrate on what seemed a far more important challenge, namely, to discover what the pianist proposed to play. He always derived pleasure from such anticipation and sometimes even took the score with him and tried to follow the artist's interpretation.

Much to his annoyance there didn't seem to be any of the usual elderly female programme-sellers on duty in the foyer. Presumably someone from the management would make the announcements, or even the artist himself might pass comment, as Lev Pouishnoff used to do. In any case, Winslett knew most items in the standard repertoire and was rarely unable to identify even the encores.

He fumbled for the ticket but he could not find it anywhere on the ground and a search through his pockets yielded only his bus ticket from Streatham Hill. He cursed his own carelessness, but happily his ticketless state didn't seem to matter though there was no usher ready to shepherd him to a seat. He was a little perturbed by the absence of people like himself, seasoned music-lovers of both sexes, waiting to go in. He squinted at his watch – almost 7.45. Could he possibly have been first on the scene? He headed for the double doors barring the interior of the hall. His steps echoed unusually loudly on the paved flooring.

Inside it was almost dark. As soon as he passed through the pains in his head intensified. The rows of seats on either side of the aisle were empty. The lighting in the main body of the hall was off and the platform with the Steinway grand, open and ready, was shrouded in gloom. Winslett had heard that some pianists preferred this – Richter for instance, whose keyboard was illuminated only by a single forty-watt bulb and Themeli the blind Greek whose natural affliction gave him no choice – and concluded that Dragorin had chosen in this way not to have his concentration disturbed.

It was also evident that not only were the conventional pre-liminaries missing but also that the audience had not yet arrived. The hall was silent, with not a rustle, not a cough to indicate the presence of an expectant public. But as he started to walk down he became aware of a substantial presence. Glancing behind him he noticed a soundless crowd following him in. Their sudden appearance and the fact that his eyes were slipping in and out of focus made him even more anxious. Where could they have come from, so many and all at once, almost as if they had mate-rialised out of the nether regions.

Winslett quickened his unsteady pace down the central aisle. The seats bore no numbers and he felt a strong objection, almost a revulsion, to sitting in close proximity to any of these late arrivals, a distaste which deepened as he became aware of un-pleasant shuffling sounds and a rustling of clothing.

Winslett found himself at the end of the front row, the only person to be seated there. This too was a strange thing, consider-ing the abrupt arrival of a large audience. He tried to look back over his shoulder and satisfy his curiosity but it was as if he had suddenly developed a frozen neck, as a dreamer, trying to run, loses the use of his legs. In fact, it was as if he had begun to live in a fantastic dream, like the poet of *Kubla Khan*, submerged in a drug-induced trance of artistic creation. Although he knew he was in the familiar Woolgar Hall surroundings, waiting, as he had so often done, for the performing artist to emerge and take his place on the stage, Winslett recognised a novel abnormality in his present situation and was gripped by eerie feelings of apprehension. Something markedly out-of-the ordinary was happening or about to happen. Of that he was certain.

His neck was quite painful and he did not dare to turn it, From somewhere far back to his rear came a faint sound of applause, which gradually grew louder and louder. After such a slow start the auditorium must surely be filled to maximum capacity, Winslett decided and found himself joining in, anticipating the pianist's imminent arrival. Almost immediately the ovation behind him abruptly ceased and Winslett, realising with embarrassment that he was applauding alone, settled back to enjoy the recital.

When it came, the artist's appearance was like a conjuring trick. One moment the stage was empty, the next, suddenly he was there, an indistinct, thinnish personage, face blurred, crouched over the instrument and without any conventional preliminaries bringing enormous bony hands down to strike the keys. The volume of sound he produced filled the hall, at first distantly, with a strange regular tempo in the bass and a merging discord in the treble, gradually becoming louder and more incisive as fragments of scattered themes gradually came together to establish a recognisable 3/4 waltz rhythm.

From its clouded *pianissimo* opening Winslett immediately identified the work as Maurice Ravel's 'poéme choreographique' *La Valse*, an enigmatic re-creation of the atmosphere of the Viennese court in the 1850s. The work is open to interpretation in the context of the gradual collapse of Europe's stability in the First World War. Loss of her traditional security is echoed in the swirling waltz themes, one upon the next, and mounting in jagged stages to a daring nerve-shattering climax, more simply understood as a musical symbol of violent death at the end of a carefree life.

Winslett knew it well in its original orchestral version recorded by Ansermet and the Paris Conservatoire Orchestra. As a piano solo it was less familiar though perhaps more revealing of detail and the composer's four-handed reduction was not often performed. To bring it off on a solo instrument demanded a master and the listening Winslett knew within seconds that he was now in the presence of such a one. Not since he had heard Rachmaninoff at the Queen's Hall in 1938 had he been so transported.

But who was this "one" poised at the keyboard? The renowned Ilya Dragorin, presumably. Winslett had never seen him, not even in a photograph. This thin figure looked alien, unfriendly, threatening even, with its hairless dome and flattish nose. In silhouette against the light the face did look something like a death's head – but what light? Winslett could make out no source of illumination on the platform, yet the instrument glowed faintly, as if phosphorescent. The Viennese waltz tempo was now clearly marked and it was easy to for him to imagine the aristocratic dancers and their ladies revolving in the vast ballroom, urged on to still faster rhythms by the imperial orchestra, ringing out a series of triumphal major chords before crumpling into a *melange* of mock-waltz tunes in a variety of keys.

Such a violent development cast a dark shadow over the imaginary ballroom, a shadow which threatened to change the celebratory pomp of the occasion into a chaos of uncertainty. The composer's genius revealed the gyrating pairs gradually losing control as they were drawn helplessly into the clutches of an irresistible daemonic force. The succession of broken *fortissimo* chords which signalled the abandonment of gaiety and a headlong descent of the doomed couples into the abyss, rivetted

Winslett to his seat as the final flourish crashed out and contrasting total silence followed.

The pianist rose from his instrument and bowed. Winslett started to applaud but suddenly realised that he was again entirely alone in his gesture of appreciation. Behind him only dead silence reigned, with not even a rustle to indicate the presence of others. Had they all gone? A wave of terror engulfed him and he struggled in vain to see who or what had gathered behind. The gloom had intensified and the luminosity around the instrument was fading fast. He sensed that the lean figure of the pianist was looking directly at him and it was in that moment that what he had recently read and forgotten about Ilya Dragorin flooded into his mind – a brief notice in that morning's paper. This brilliant performance could not have been given by Ilya Dragorin because Ilya Dragorin had just died!

The pianist stepped down from the platform and for a brief moment his bony features were caught by the last flicker of light. Winslett closed his eyes to banish the eyeless stare of the musician, an alien personage of whose identity he was now beginning to be assured and made a frenzied attempt to drag his leaden limbs out of the seat. His head was splitting and a magnetic force drew him towards the platform as the black shape of the pianist seemed to grow until it towered over him.

"No, not me", he screamed as successive shafts of icy stifling cold reached viciously into every part of his body. He felt close to suffocation and growing panic overtook him as his respiration began to fail and his will to survive dwindled.

"Surely this is the end" he murmured, "*La Valse* finishes in a swift descent to death". His own death?

The piano started again, initially as if from a long distance away but closing in on Winslett's failing consciousness. He realised that he was now hearing a version of another work, the

Mephisto Waltz of Franz Liszt, but the tinny piano sound was now raucous and out-of-tune, representing a clumsy parody of a serious performance, a jeering encore, reverberating to the high ceiling.

Winslett's tortured ears rejected it. Some remnant of his fast-shrinking connection with the real world outside the hall told him that this ghastly cacophony must surely be designed to drag him into another dimension, a grotesque musical version of Hell. He lurched to his feet, limbs still lead-like and as he twisted his painful neck round to face the exit he perceived that the rows of seats on both sides of the aisle were empty.

Muttering incoherently, Winslett stumbled up the aisle in frantic flight from that fearful tuneless jangle, hands wildly outstretched, mouthing a crude supplication to an unknown and previously unacknowledged deity.

The way to the exit was longer than he remembered it and his painful progress was impeded by invisible obstacles and what felt like uneven marshy ground into which his heavy feet sank deeper with every step. Now the piano had broken into wild *arpeggi*, threatening to claw him back to the depths of the hall. His unsteady gait was forced into the furious waltz tempo as he struggled to keep his balance against the swaying of what turned into a writhing mass of dancers pouring out of the gloom. The rows of seats had gone, leaving a vast cavern. A hideous cackle of laughter pierced what little remained of his sensibility as he was grabbed round the waist by invisible hands and pulled again and again into a pirouetting travesty of the waltz to spin round and round in a vortex until blackness blotted out the frightful din.

The next thing Winslett knew was the shaking motion of an ambulance carrying him to Paddington Hospital, unnaturally cold, freezing in every limb, slipping in and out of consciousness and stricken by panic. The attendants had to hold him down while they assured him that he was not in hell. In fact he had been found lying on the pavement in Wigmore Street. A curious crowd had quickly gathered around him.

Luckily no time had been wasted in getting help but it had been a near thing. Even in that humid July evening his body-temperature had dropped to a level barely able to support life and he had exhibited many of the classic signs of exposure. His only external injury was a broken collar-bone, apparently sustained when he fell and certainly painful enough to affect him through his dream.

At first puzzled, the hospital doctors called Winslett's condition a rare case of cryogenic stroke from which with the proper care and attention he would recover. They treated him as for a severe heart-attack and discharged him after ten days with the usual textbook warnings.

When Winslett improved sufficiently to relate his weird visionary experience to his saviours they shrugged their shoulders and agreed that the imagination was a funny thing, especially when touched off by the stress which affects everybody these days. An American psychiatrist came to the ward and took copious notes for a proposed article in a medical journal. He was especially intrigued by Winslett's insistence that the mysterious offer of a ticket had come from an American. Had he any connections with the United States?

Winslett had never been to America. But the facts of the matter stood against him. No concert had been advertised for that evening and no tickets issued. The hall had been closed. Passers-by had noticed him leaning against the bolted and barred outside door and falling down in a faint, upon which somebody had telephoned for an ambulance.

On admission their patient had been extremely agitated and talked about falling ill at a concert. Why he had conjured up Ilya

Dragorin to be his illusory pianist was easily explained. Ilya Dragorin had recently died. It had been in all the papers.

Faced by this formidable argument, Winslett reluctantly had to concede that he must take a more rational view of his condition and eat more regular meals. His wristwatch had unaccountably stopped precisely at 7.45. so that the entire episode could have lasted only a moment. I knew that a "long" dream is said to have a very short duration when measured in real time. As soon as he was allowed to leave he set out to examine back numbers of the leading dailies but in none of them did he find the notice that had allured and now eluded him.

The official *Times* obituary, however was not so elusive. It had been published while he had lain comatose in the hospital and coincidentally or not related to the very day of Winslett's "accident". Ilya Dragorin had died of a heart seizure in the middle of an afternoon recital in Carnegie Hall, New York City while playing Liszt's *Mephisto Waltz*. Winslett remembered that in his "dream" he had suddenly become aware that Dragorin was dead. The sinister significance of the international time difference in this context was not lost on Winslett, nor on me for that matter when I went to see him after he was discharged.

I never met Winslett again. Two months later I heard that the poor chap had collapsed and died in the foyer of the *Salle Gaveau*, a venue for piano concerts in Paris and exactly the place he might have chosen for his final moments. I never did find out who was playing or what was on the programme.

5. *The Egg of the Gonzu*

Fifty years ago, when a small Caribbean island which I shall call Lacrasia was still a British colony, one of her newest residents was a haggard-looking man with a pronounced limp. His identity papers introduced him to the Lacrasian Immigration authorities as Doktor Max Uhlir, a Czech herpetologist and a refugee from both Nazism and Communism. On the strength of having once been Extraordinary (Associate) Professor in his own country, Max had come to take up the relatively lowly post of Senior Demonstrator in the Zoology Department at Lacrasia's lately established University College.

His formal application for the vacancy had been based entirely upon his own statement, since his personal references and paper credentials were no longer extant. The name of Uhlir had carried some weight in zoological circles, however. In the thirties the Professor had travelled extensively in Africa, India and South-East Asia, studying the world's most deadly reptiles, but his papers on the Tic Palonga or Russell's Viper, the Black Mamba and the Krait had never been published. Their typescripts had been destroyed during the Second World War, but in a lecture given in 1938, Doktor Max had revealed that the most important of all his unpublished monographs concerned his discovery of the mysterious Gonzu, which he was rewriting from memory.

Professor Uhlir's espousal of the gonzu had been something of a joke among his pre-war colleagues. He had even bestowed his own name on it, "*serpens mirabilis Max*", and a short preliminary account of his discovery of this menacing serpent had appeared in a popular Prague newspaper in the autumn of 1938. The gonzu was, in his own words, a super-snake that had evolved with unique supernatural powers. In size, he said, it was huge, even dwarfing the Hamadryad or King Cobra. Like the cobra, the gonzu was oviparous, but whereas a cobra's egg might contain up to a score of babies with poison glands fully developed at birth, the egg of the gonzu produced only one. This snake, he wrote, was extremely rare and an obscure habitat in the impenetrable rainforests of Brazil had ensured its survival. By sheer luck, he announced, he had found a gonzu egg intact but refused to produce it before the publication of his monograph, an eccentricity he justified on the ground of "academic security" and a current wave of plagiarism.

A cobra's strike was, he would explain to the uninitiated, neurotoxic, resulting in respiratory arrest which rapidly brought about a comatose descent to a certain death, unless an antidote could be quickly administered, but to the strike of the gonzu no antidote existed.

Serpens mirabilis Max was known as "The Ghost Snake" by natives dwelling along the banks of the Amazon because of its astonishing power of camouflage which rendered it nearly invisible and its speed of attack, which ensured that no victim could survive for long enough to tell the tale of an encounter with the phantom. In fact, as Professor Pichler, the Dean of his Faculty pointed out, no-one seemed to have seen this "wonderful serpent" or its egg except Doktor Max himself who resisted Pichler's demands to produce tangible evidence. When Pichler finally called him a liar a Board of Enquiry was set up to investigate the ethics of the case.

The Board never met. A few weeks afterwards, Czechoslovakia was annexed by Hitler and the gonzu and its egg were forgotten. Professor Max lost his job and was replaced by one of his own students, a Nazi sympathiser. Sent to a labour camp, no more was heard of him until the war's end. No more, that is, until a stateless person named Max Uhlir arrived in London in the summer of 1948, a refugee from the Communist coup. One legacy from his years in the labour camp was his bad limp, caused, he said, by a brutal SS officer named Alois Dorfmann, who used him as a subject for a conjuring trick that went wrong. He swore that one day he would exact retribution from this Dorfmann, who had disappeared after the war.

Max's account of his travails was a familiar one among academics who had fallen foul of totalitarian regimes. After the 1945 liberation from the Nazis thanks to former colleagues like the collaborator Pichler, still Dean of the Faculty, Max was denied his old job. He travelled to London and managed to find work in the Reptile House at the Regent's Park Zoo. After numerous unsuccessful petitions based on his unpublished papers and claims of work-in-progress on the gonzu his plight was sympathetically considered and through the good offices of the international academic network a junior post was secured for him at the newly-opened College in Lacrasia.

At first he was grateful for the opportunity to return to his profession but gradually resentment at the lowered status set in. This condition was aggravated by certain of his English colleagues who waggishly addressed him as "Herr Doktor Professor" in tones of exaggerated politeness and made clumsy jokes about snakes in general and "Max's wonderful serpent" in particular. He much preferred the keen Caribbean students who listened intently to his yarns on fieldwork in the Amazon Basin and with rather less interest to his obsessive denunciations of Dorfmann, who had apparently once acted as assistant to the notorious Kalanag, a stage magician popular with the leading Nazis. Dorfmann's idea of fun was to make prisoners participate in his experiments with new tricks.

Max also resented his treatment outside the College. So near to the end of the Second World War it was tempting for Lacrasian residents of the older generation to identify "Doktors" with gutteral accents as highly questionable figures who had somehow escaped justice to pursue their evil ways in a British colony. The recently-established University College was not popular with old-school colonial residents, who regarded it less as an admirable example of social progress than as a font of subversion. Its lush campus was regularly accused of harbouring crypto-communists and other undesirables poised to take over as soon as Lacrasia achieved her political independence. In their view Max Uhlir, if no longer a Nazi, was at least a crypto-Communist, a keeper of poisonous snakes waiting to loose them on the island. People like him should be deported at once. His application to join the Country Club was unsuccessful.

In the spring of 1949 an unsigned letter was received by the national newspaper, *The Daily Lacrasian*, accusing Doktor Uhlir of importing a gonzu egg from Brazil which had since hatched and adding some frightening details of the single baby's capabilities. Subsequent correspondence from readers included a contradictory statement from a retired Indian Army Major. This gentleman described the gonzu as "purely mythical, like the dragon" but feared by the superstitious natives of the Amazon Basin as a creature owning supernatural powers. In his opinion, reported sightings had probably been long-distance views of an anaconda, a large constrictor, dangerous but not poisonous, which could grow to thirty feet in length.

Doktor Max responded to the Major in a lengthy diatribe which emphasised his own singular role as the discoverer of the gonzu a decade earlier. It was no myth. His monograph, he assured his readers, would have made him an *Ordinarius* or "full Professor" had it been published. Bewailing his loss of career,

Doktor Max expressed his gratitude to Lacrasia for enabling him to recover it. He hoped to continue his research on the gonzu but hastened to reassure those concerned that no live examples would ever be introduced to corrupt the idyllic wildlife of the country. As for the egg, the only serpent egg he possessed was that of an Indian cobra more than ten years old, which could not possibly hatch. He kept it in a glass case on the mantelpiece in his one-bedroom flat on the campus and occasionally brought it to the laboratory to show his students.

Doktor Max did not need to ask who had sent the original anonymous letter to the paper. He had written it himself.

The Maria Monkhouse Professor of Zoology, Rupert McKenna, a smooth-talking Dubliner under whose immediate auspices the Czech held his temporary post, was unwilling to commit himself and told a press representative that the study of dangerous reptiles was never his speciality – that was why Doktor Uhlir, a scientist of the highest integrity, had been recommended by the colonial authority in London. So far as he knew the egg was that of an Indian cobra but to avoid further argument Doktor Uhlir had promised to donate it to the island's Museum.

The Doktor had made no such promise but under the circumstances he pretended to accept Professor McKenna's solution. An uneasy peace on the campus lasted over the week-end, until an excited student, a Miss Ruby Wynter, rushed into Professor McKenna's office with the alarming news that she had seen "with her own eyes a nasty-looking greenish snake" coiled round the branch of a tree by the University Chapel not five minutes before.

A worried Professor McKenna said that it was probably just a grass snake but the attractive Miss Wynter was not to be denied. Grass snakes did not climb trees. This monster was too long and evil. It frightened her.

Professor McKenna pursued the problem of identity. Could it be a Lacrasian cobra? This was nothing like an Indian or Egyptian cobra but a short, fat yellow rat-snake peculiar to the island. Though not harmful to man it was feared by the rural populace and killed on sight without mercy. No, definitely greenish, not yellow, said Miss Wynter, a promising candidate for Honours in Psychology. Then she dropped her bombshell. Had a gonzu been hatched after all?

Like many members of his profession, Rupert McKenna was a man-of-action *manqué*. He quickly donned leggings and thick leather boots, got out the .38 Webley which in his capacity of Major in the Lacrasian Militia he kept loaded at all times and declared a state of emergency in the Faculty. Classes were halted and a curious crowd of students assembled. Led by the Professor they proceeded cautiously to the Chapel where Miss Wynter pointed at the tree where she had seen the snake.

Sure enough, the reptile was there in plain sight, exactly as she had described it, "nasty-looking and greenish", wound around a low branch.

Motioning the others to stay well back, the Professor crept forward, drew his gun, aimed carefully and fired several shots, whereupon fragments of rubber and cotton stuffing flew into the air and the amazed group of spectators nervously began to snigger.

Miss Ruby Wynter, who chose this vital moment to leave the scene, was later observed laughing hysterically in the company of a group of male students, one of whom, an undersized fellow named Fitzroy Greaves, happened to be the editor of the student newspaper. Professor McKenna was furious when a dramatic account of the episode appeared in the issue following, accompanied by a cartoon in which he was depicted in a cowboy hat waving a gun at an obviously stuffed snake with the words "GOTCHA GONZU!"

More reports of sightings started to come in. A labourer had fainted when he saw the shadow of a huge snake on the wall of the Arts and Crafts Centre and a female member of the administrative staff had hysterics when something wriggled up a palm tree outside her office. It was, she said, black with yellow markings and hissed.

Man's primitive fear was awakened; news of a potentially lethal snake on the loose spread rapidly through the campus and after a series of lurid reports in the tabloid *Evening Comet*, over the entire island. The *Comet's* leading article described how a Mr Roosevelt Roach, a music student on his way to practise on the University Chapel organ had observed a slimy trail leading from the door to the music bench and smelled a fetid odour. The writer attributed this to the recent presence of a large snake and congratulated Mr Roach on his good luck in not having got there earlier.

This was picked up by *The Daily Lacrasian* which announced that if the reptile's venom was neurotoxic, Mr Roach had indeed been lucky, since a victim of its bite might be dead in fifteen minutes or survive for several hours, depending on his physical health. Doktor Max, known to his students as one of the few men to have survived a bite from a banded coral snake, wrote to the paper saying that if his assailant had been a gonzu, the student organist would have been dead in less than seconds.

The reigning Principal, Sir Thomas Short, a lawyer-politician recently knighted and exported from England to smooth the path prior to the granting of full University status to the College decreed, with the aid of a quotation from *Paradise Lost,* that until the guilty serpent was caught and killed, Doktor Max Uhlir's laboratory must close. He warned students that further practical jokes would not be tolerated. An area around the Chapel was roped off and volunteers assisted the police to make a search of the building.

No snake was found, but the partially-eaten body of a goat was. Its corpse was taken to the hospital and examined to find the cause of the animal's demise, which was not snakebite but strangulation. Attention was soon drawn to a likely culprit from the serpent family, Boris the boa, who obligingly turned up fast asleep behind the organ.

Lacrasia boasted a small Zoo, nestling inside the Queen's Gardens on the north-eastern edge of the island's capital, but with one exception only indigenous animals were kept there. The Curator, Hans Klima, a refugee from Austria, had become a friend of Doktor Max. His collection of caged reptiles was non-venomous and included Boris, a reticulated python, a young constrictor of ten feet in length who at a pinch, or rather a squeeze, could have choked a helpless animal.

The discovery of the dead goat coincided with the Curator's complaint that some mischief-maker had released Boris from his cage. The Zoo was at least a mile from the campus and it was obvious that Boris must have had transport. Max Uhlir and Hans Klima agreed that the slimy trail in the Chapel was undoubtedly his, and Boris was returned to his cage.

The Daily Lacrasian ignored the unpromising Boris story and kept up the pressure on the wider public by asking if The Enemy was a single adult or the multiple result of a hatched egg and suggesting that people living in the vicinity of the College shake out their shoes before putting them on since baby snakes liked dark, warm places.

At this stage in the gonzu saga a man in his forties named as Everard Corliss on his Argentine passport entered Lacrasia. Corliss was a well-known professional magician resident in

Buenos Aires who performed under the stage-name Medellin. At the height of the gonzu panic, he was staying at one of the luxury hotels hastily erected on Lacrasia's North Coast to accommodate the post-war wave of tourists from North America brought in by cruise ships and the newly-established air lines. Interviewed and photographed as a visiting celebrity, the magician was asked by a *Comet* reporter to comment on this dangerous reptile which was spreading such terror throughout the island. Didn't he live in South America? Did such a creature exist? Was there no way to get rid of the scourge?

Corliss/Medellin had never heard of the gonzu but was quick to see a golden opportunity arising and smartly recited Hamlet's words about there being more things in heaven and earth than the Dane's old friend Horatio could know in his philosophy. Warming to his theme, he suggested that the spirit of the gonzu might be exorcised by "one with The Power and sent back to the Limbo whence it came".

"By one such as yourself?" inquired the interviewer, scenting a possible follow-up. "Could you, as a great sorcerer, be persuaded to rid us of this fiendish scourge?"

Ever open to flattery, Medellin inclined his sleek head and stroked his goatee. Here was unexpected free publicity. He rapidly weighed up the odds. He himself could put on a preliminary show of stage-magic and finish up with a grand demonstration of his own supernatural powers. Whether this gonzu existed or not, he could hardly lose. He named his fee for a single performance which, he insisted, would have to take place on the University campus haunted by the gonzu within three days. It would take him that much time to prepare himself for the ordeal.

Principal Sir Thomas Short, a complete sceptic in such matters, reluctantly agreed. A curtained stage and bleachers to seat the hoped-for large audience were set up before the administrative building.

In the meantime Doktor Max, his research outlet closed and his job newly threatened by a letter from the Dean warning him that his contract might not be renewed, considered how he could get his own back on these colonial English stuffed shirts and their local hangers-on. His anger was fuelled by the generous treatment accorded to Medellin, a vulgar publicity-seeking charlatan received as an honoured guest by Lacrasia's Country Club. The proposed exorcism of his gonzu provided a much sharper and more immediate focus for Doktor Max's obsession than the petty tyrants of the University College or the ignorant *bourgeoisie* beyond the gates.

Doktor Max was poised to sweep to his revenge.

At eight o'clock three evenings later the ticket-holders hesitantly took their places on hard wooden chairs inside a roped-off "danger" area. Several hundred occupied standing-room at a safer distance. Tropical darkness had fallen and the indigenous palm-tree-frogs had begun to sound their whistling note. The only illumination came from four ground lights ranged around the stage.

Notices had been placed in both newspapers advising spectators to wear stout shoes and thick trousers in case the exorcised gonzu became angry enough to bite. A first-aid stall was erected, with anti-snakebite serum available, though what antidote against what species of serpent was not made clear.

These were Medellin's ideas. Such precautions helped to generate a *frisson* of fear. He had learned from long experience that an audience feeling individually as well as collectively vulnerable assisted and enhanced his own performance. Many might scoff at the security arrangements and tell one another that it was all just a stunt, but few were completely free of doubts and nobody disregarded Medellin's recommendation on dress in spite of the humid evening temperature.

Nearest the stage sat Sir Thomas and Lady Short and the Deans of Faculties, with the Professors and senior administrators in the first two rows behind, every one with complimentary tickets. The Principal and his Lady occupied armchairs upon which cushions had been placed for their comfort. The Faculty of Science was out in force and the ubiquitous local pressmen and a few urban notables on special invitation completed the complement. Doktor Max had found a chair near the back. He knew what he had to do.

Gloomy music was just audible from a loudspeaker. A group of students, their faces concealed by animal masks, had brought in a large yellow-painted *papier-maché* egg on a tray. Sir Thomas scowled, consulted his watch and muttered something to Lady Short, who grimaced and lit a cigarette.

At eight-twenty-five Medellin appeared at last, crowned by a glossy top hat and wearing a black Dracula-style cloak. From past experience he knew exactly how long to stretch out this delaying period. He bowed to a polite ripple of applause and went straight into his act without vocal preliminaries. Like most successful illusionists, Medellin looked the part and did not talk. His sleight-of-hand, though conventional, was brilliant and in spite of an absence of stage props he held the spectators spellbound until nine. Only then did he speak, with a slight American accent.

"Sir President, Professors, Ladies and Gentlemen, Students", he began. "I hope you have enjoyed my magic. It gives me great pleasure to be here in your beautiful island. But some of you will know the real reason for my presence before you. Some kind people have invited me to your College for a special reason. Your President has asked me specially to appear on this stage…"

Principal Sir Thomas Short winced "… and I, Medellin, am here at his request on your behalf to banish the spirit of the gonzu from your land".

Just then came a harsh interruption in a language which most recognised as German. *"Dorfmann! Ich habe das Gonzus Ei."*

All heads turned. Medellin, visibly distracted, was at first unresponsive but when the speaker repeated his remark, snapped out impatiently, "I'm sorry sir, I don't understand. What can I do for you?"

Doktor Max smiled and limped forward. In his hand he held a bright green egg and reverting to his usual fractured English offered it to the startled Medellin, who glared down at him suspiciously.

"So … you are here to exorcise my gonzu. I am Professor Max Uhlir. I discovered the gonzu and this is his egg. I named it. *Serpens mirabilis Max.* Herr Dorfmann."

"Look here, I am Medellin. I don't know you or any Dorfmann or what your game is…" the magician called out loudly, "… unless you're trying to spoil the show for all these people?"

"Natürlich nicht, Herr Dorfmann. I'm only here to help you if you are not afraid. Are you not afraid Herr Dorfmann? Take the egg. He handed the green object to the magician, whose professional poise seemed to have deserted him.

"That is Death, Herr Dorfmann and for you Justice."

With that Doktor Max bowed and returned to his place, followed by the hostile gaze of the front two rows.

"Shut up for God's sake, Uhlir," snapped the Dean. Doktor Max bowed again and resumed his seat.

When the buzz had died down, Medellin surveyed his audience, held up the green egg and with a flourish, palmed it, made it reappear and with an uneasy smile placed it gently on his table, throwing a black cloth loosely over it.

"I have here the egg of a gonzu, a deadly serpent," he boomed. "My good friend wishes me to release the spirit of the gonzu, so first I must break its egg."

From the empty air he produced a small hammer and with a dramatic gesture brought it down sharply on the bulge in the cloth. Closing his eyes, the magician gathered his flowing cloak about him and continued in a different tone of voice, perfectly audible but high pitched and faint, as though from a distance. The words were in no language that anyone present had ever heard, a fact not surprising since Medellin had invented it only the day before.

"*Karshwalla degud vershwalla, fringa tergat moballa. Ofisti progorsi mi! Ofisti progorsi mi!*" rang out the opening lines. The audience sat open-mouthed. Medellin recited several verses, ending with the refrain "*Gonzu progorsi KARRAM!*" repeated a number of times, each time succeeded by a pause, marked by a series of spellbinding gestures from Medellin and growing in volume.

The Very Important People in the front rows sat bolt upright, frozen to their seats, jaws tightly clenched, concealing their anxieties and uncertain as to whether this strange demonstration was just a piece of showmanship or a serious attempt to call up the fabulous gonzu. Suddenly from the rear appeared a busty girl in a sequinned outfit wearing a Devil mask and when Medellin completed his litany – *Matumba konchetkum gonzu ... KARRAM!* – the she-devil lit a fuse hanging down from the painted egg.

With a loud bang it burst, firing a swarm of brilliant phosphorescent shapes high into the air, accompanied by a succession of detonations.

This impressive display came as a surprise to the audience, including Max, but not to Medellin who had that morning "hatched" the egg with the help of an assistant in the chemistry laboratory. The magician had paid him and the student group well for their services. Spectators familiar with pre-war Guy Fawkes' Nights ought to have recognised the spectacular effects of a firework labelled "Mine of Serpents", which disgorged a luminous assortment of undulating shapes in vibrant greens, reds and yellows, which lit up the night sky and climaxed in a lavish cascade of twisting silver arrows.

Medellin doffed his top hat and bowed.

"*KARRAM!* Behold, myriads of baby gonzus had been called forth and made to vanish into the air!"

He breathed a sigh of relief. So much for the "exorcism". He, Medellin, had done what he had promised, more or less, and after they'd had a minute to recover, the audience would, as usual, recognise his genius with their applause. Later they might realise that all they had seen was clever showmanship and an entertaining firework display but by then he would be on a flight to Miami with his dollar cheque.

Doktor Max waited. The various tricks he had perpetrated with the willing help of students – the dummy snake, the slimy trail in the Chapel, the removal of Boris and goat from the Zoo with the connivance of Hans Klima – had bred hysteria on the campus. He had not expected this spectacular example of *feux d'artifice* which seemed to have benefited Medellin, but Max knew that his own small contribution to the show had yet to play its part.

The front rows started to clap intermittently but most remained dumbly immobile until the last of the "serpents" had spluttered out. The ground lights had failed, leaving only the candles to illuminate the stage, but people could see that something was puzzling Medellin. Attracted by a movement under the cloth, after a moment's hesitation he gingerly lifted one corner and then whipped the whole of it away.

"Dorfmann! Serpens mirabilis Max!" shouted Doktor Max, running forward. His limp seemed to have gone.

Members of the audience differed in their accounts of what they could remember from that awful moment when what looked like a sinuous smoky shape reared up from the table and shot upwards into the magician's face, clouding it with a white mist which billowed out over the stage and dissolved. Applause marked appreciation at what the watchers thought was another clever trick until Medellin fell against the curtained backdrop, bringing it down, its folds covering his writhing body. He made no sound and in seconds he was still. The girl in the devil mask threw it off and revealed herself as Ruby Wynter. Someone produced a flashlight and in its beam those nearest saw that Medellin's contorted face had shrivelled to half its normal size.

Lady Short screamed and the crowd surged forward as her husband and confused officials sought to control the panic. When order had been to some degree restored a doctor fetched from the University Hospital pronounced Medellin dead but refused to speculate on the cause.

His doubt was carried forward to the inquest. Doktor Max, a nervous witness, kept on doggedly insisting that the real name of the deceased was not Everard Corliss but Alois Dorfmann. He told the police that the spirit of the gonzu must have lain dormant inside the cobra's egg until Medellin's attempt at exorcism had aroused it, but no-one believed such a fanciful tale. It seemed that Max had a strong motive and opportunity and it was tempting to accept the deadly gonzu as his means. But of material evidence suggesting the presence of a snake there remained only a shattered eggshell and several conflicting stories from witnesses close to the stage. Miss Wynter was sure that she had seen a giant python shooting out of the egg like a bullet. Fitzroy Greaves claimed only to have been aware of a long shadow flickering momentarily under a dim light. In the end the coroner's jury put Medellin's death down to heart failure caused by a sudden shock.

Sir Thomas Short, an admirer of Agatha Christie, offered the court an ingenious solution. Far from being enemies, Max and the magician had joined forces to ensure the success of the so-called "exorcism". Their apparently hostile exchange had been a device for handing over the egg. Memories of his treatment in the labour-camp by Dorfmann had no doubt given Doktor Uhlir reason to hate him but he was now far away and had nothing to do with the tragedy. The Principal concluded that both Doktor Uhlir and Corliss-Medellin wished, though for different reasons, to encourage faith in the existence of this mythical reptile. Unfortunately Medellin had died at the climax of a species of trick which any competent conjurer could duplicate. Max hotly denied this rational explanation but for those who did not believe in ghosts it was a plausible one.

Obituaries in the international press outlined Corliss's stage career, which had taken him all over the United States and Latin America but, because of the war, never to Europe. The shadowy Dorfmann had disappeared in 1945 and was thought to have fled to Paraguay. The Americans turned up a blurred photograph which suggested that the former SS officer might have borne a strong facial resemblance to Corliss, perhaps close enough to inspire a slightly unbalanced Max Uhlir to plot a misguided revenge which, fortunately for him, had gone no further than a public demonstration based on his long obsession with a non-existent poisonous snake. Max denied this as well. For him Corliss and Dorfmann were the same person and the gonzu had served the cause of justice.

A Lacrasian jury recommended that no attention be paid to this aspect of the tragedy and exonerated Max from any direct responsibility while strongly recommending his deportation as an undesirable. A verdict of death from natural causes was recorded on Corliss-Medellin, a decision which satisfied no-one who had seen him die.

Sir Thomas Short was delighted to send Max a letter terminating his contract *"for reasons of health"* but the aggrieved Doktor had already left the island. A few months later Mr Fitzroy Greaves and Miss Ruby Wynter each received an unsigned postcard from the Amazon Basin inscribed with three words in Latin and a neatly-executed sketch of a forked-tongued serpent emerging from an egg.

The Daily Lacrasian muddied the waters still further when under the caption "So Who Was He?" its front page carried a statement 'from a foreign correspondent' alleging that the Czech herpetologist Professor Max Uhlir had died from typhus in 1944.

6. *Marietta*

Guide-books to Sicily cautiously recommend the *Catacombe Cappuccini* on the south-western outskirts of Palermo; cautiously since squeamish tourists have on occasion shown distaste for the rows of fleshless skulls and mummified corpses preserved by embalmers against the remorseless ravages of centuries. However, nearly all visitors find that the eight thousand permanent occupants, spaced out in a vast charnel-house hewn from volcanic rock beneath the *Convento*, are not to be feared.

But are exceptions not said to prove the rule? John Crest, London solicitor, convalescing after a nervous breakdown and armed with his beloved camera, crossed the Piazza Cappuccini and descended the concrete steps leading to the catacombs. With only thirty minutes left before official closing-time he rapidly ran the gauntlet of anonymous monkish skeletons peering down from their niches and arrived in the hindmost section of this well-ordered Palermitan estate which harboured the crypt's most notable secular residents divided, in death as in life, by status. Ordinary *Uomini* were separated from *Dottori in Medicina*, *Professori* and *Avocati*, and from *Donne*, *Bambini* and *Virgini*. Some inmates reposed in stone coffins, others, strung up by wire, stood rigidly at attention. The higher ranks of this bourgeois elite retained recognisable physical features, preserved in arsenic, vinegar or quicklime, attired in the sartorial fashions of their day and identified by handwritten labels.

Contrary to his expectations, the Englishman found the spectacle pathetic rather than disturbing. Youth, cut off even before its prime, and revered age were represented. Here was a boy of fourteen, Giuseppe Siciliano, *morto 1851*, looking up respectfully at *Dottore* Giacchino Distefano D'Alia, *morto 26 Ottobre 1880*. 'Physician, heal thyself,' mused Crest, turning with greater curiosity to the latest arrival, an infant, in her hair a yellow bow and identifed as *Rosalia Lombardo nata 1918 – morta 1920, GB imbalsamata*. 'Imbalsamata' meant embalmed. Crest was aware that in 1881 Garibaldi had made the embalming process illegal so that Rosalia, named after Palermo's patron saint, must have been an exception, *Mafiosi* permitting, or on second thoughts wasn't it the Camorra, the Black Hand, that ran things in Sicily in those days?

The child Rosalie slumbered peacefully, enclosed in a miniature glass coffin, an icon of innocence. Though it at first repelled him, Crest exclaimed aloud in genuine admiration of this truly remarkable example of the embalmer's skill. This "GB" had been an artist of the first rank, who had all but restored the child to life. She appeared newly asleep but in the full vibrancy of life. Nothing of death was there. The skin, the flesh, the features, her auburn curls crowned by a yellow bow, a beguiling picture of innocence, the legendary Sleeping Beauty, waiting for the Prince to awaken her. The sheer perfection of the image and the glaring incongruity of the situation banished baser thoughts from his mind.

Just at that moment, Crest sensed, rather than felt, the touch of a hand on his arm. Irritated and thinking that he was the target of a pickpocket, a type of dishonest citizen by no means unknown in Palermo's crowded places, the Englishman turned to discover the source of his annoyance but saw no-one close at hand – only the figure of a old gentleman in a cape and a black shovel hat such as Italian priests wore, retreating down the aisle leading to the rearmost part of the cavern.

A group of Japanese tourists chattered excitedly and pointed at the dead child. A shiver ran down Crest's spine but reason soon asserted itself and he stood back patiently as they levelled their cameras. There seemed to be no objection to free photography in the convent of the Capuchins.

In the midst of these historical ruminations Crest became aware of a fellow in a dark suit selling picture-postcards of the inmates. Might as well save film, he decided and was about to offer money when a card was pushed into his hand from behind. Before Crest could turn around to question the donor of this singular favour, his benefactor had slipped away and vanished from view.

Crest opened his hand to discover what he was clutching, expecting to find an advertisement for some local *pizzeria* but it turned out to be an original sketch of a young woman in a reclining position, her physical charms prominently and rather coarsely displayed. The drawing was crude in itself but the unknown artist had caught an elusive and subtly sinister quality in his sitter. The Englishman would have taken it to signify an offer of a different kind had it not been for an inscription in crabbed handwriting, *Marietta, GB imbalsamata*. He placed it in his wallet.

A bell sounded to indicate that it was time for visitors to head for the exit. In the light of later events Crest would have been well advised to heed the bell and return to the outside world, but the cumulative effect of his odd encounters within the *Convento* and the inexplicable influence which seemed to be encouraging his interest in this shadowy "GB" banished any hesitation which in a less curious man might have stopped further investigation. He consulted his watch, saw it was almost five and gave vent to a mild expletive as a second bell sounded to summon stragglers.

Reluctant to abandon his quest, he hurriedly looked about to find a guide who might direct him to this second example of GB's impeccable restoration and spotted a recess at the far end of the last aisle from which a thin personage wearing a black top-hat and swathed in shabby clothes too big for him was just emerging. This individual pointed back into the narrow alcove and Crest, telling himself that this was yet another signal not to be ignored, squeezed past with a muttered "con permesso". The fellow, whose features under the hat Crest did not care to look at, reeked of a mixture of garlic and some other pungent odour which the Englishman was unable to identify.

Crest found himself in a gloomy vestibule which widened after a few yards to reveal a transparent enclosure. That last visitor had left traces of his presence hanging in the dry air, but Crest abruptly forgot such an unsavoury intrusion when, peering through the misty glass, he beheld a female figure reclining on the far side of a red plush couch wide enough for two. She was obviously the original of the drawing. At first glance he was sure that the woman, like the child Rosalia, was alive. Her dark tresses shone even in the poor light, her pink flesh was flawless, her body the very acme of the voluptuous and luxurious. The undulating line of her ripe form was accentuated by a diaphanous garment that barely hid the shadowy area between her inviting thighs. Again, like the child Rosalia, she seemed just to be lightly asleep.

Suffice to say that this middle-aged bachelor was instantaneously transfixed, transported, and transmogrified, his dormant erotic appetites revivified at the sight of this faultless image of female pulchritude barred from his trembling hands only by the glass. Attached to the latter was a faded label in an old-style script, bearing the legend *Marietta nata 4 Marzo 1864 morta 12 Aprile 1888 per GB imbalsamata* and three lines of verse:

natura insegna a noi temer la morte
ma amor poi mirabilament face
suave a suoi qual ch'e ad ogni altro amaro

Crest knew enough Italian to understand the drift of the poet's message, in effect that whoever lives for love first voluntarily dies to everything else and has no natural fear of death as a barrier. Later he found out that they came from a sonnet by the fifteenth-century Florentine Lorenzo de Medici. Lorenzo's disciples would have understood Crest's passion. Most normal men conceal in their mind's eye an image of womanly perfection – the Platonic Vision of Eros, signifying an unreachable ideal of feminine allure, its imperfect earthly reflection condemned by the misogynous mediaeval Church as a blatant symbol of sexual temptation.

The seductive Marietta became in a trice Crest's personal Vision of Eros incarnate. He stood erect, caught in a sudden irresistible wave of fleshly concupiscence, his physical sensibilities inflamed by an unaccustomed tumescence. His longings burst out spontaneously into words, dictated by an uncontrollable force outside himself and echoing the sentiment of Lorenzo's poem.

"O Marietta, I could love you unto death!"

His heart pounded and he exuded sweat from every pore. For an immeasurable moment he was stunned and unable to stir. But ecstasy is of its nature fleeting. Lorenzo's dead mistress had been the Florentine's enchanted worldly version of the peace of divine repose but Crest, a lapsed Catholic who adhered to no religious faith, recognised even in the midst of his euphoria that what had touched him contained nothing of divinity but possibly much of the Devil. For Crest, as for all normal men, association with such an extreme perversion as necrophilia was unutterably loathsome. In a flash his lust turned to self-contempt.

Realization of the viler source of this cursed appetite for immediate physical relief burst in on his reverie and overwhelmed this ageing lawyer with feelings of shame and disgust. He felt sick. The spell was shattered, all desire left him and he turned away. But for a moment he hesitated. Should he let his photographer's instincts move him to capture on film a record of his near descent to corruption?

Steadying himself he focussed his camera on the glass. The flash caused the flimsily-swathed form of Marietta to shimmer in the brief harsh light almost as if she were gathering herself to rise up. Crest, a horrid chill running down his spine, lost his balance and lurched forward against the glass. In that second he became conscious of a presence behind him and, confused by the intrusion, averted his gaze from the beguiling but treacherous temptress recumbent in her glass tomb to receive the fleeting impression of a tall hat silhouetted in the entrance, accompanied by a fresh gust of that pervasive acerbic stench.

Submerged in a torrent of fears and emotions, Crest stumbled out of the dark into the illuminated area of the catacombs in near panic. Tall Hat had somehow vanished into the throng of visitors but that disquieting aroma seemed to pursue the Englishman on his frantic course towards the steps leading to the exit.

It was with a pounding heart and a great feeling of relief that he found himself outside in the *Piazza* in the midst of a noisy group of young Germans. One asked if he was ill. Nervously he glanced around him, but of his malodorous stalker he thankfully saw no sign. He glanced at his watch and saw with a start that it was exactly five o'clock. How long had he been in that awful place? One minute, two? So-called "long" dreams were said to be in reality of very brief duration. Had he really been there at all?

On the nearby *Piazza Danisinni* he discovered a cheerful café and ordered a Campari-soda, which helped him to bring his hard-headed legal training to bear on this alarming brush with the seeming supernatural, largely, he convinced himself, the product of a lively imagination working amid macabre surroundings. With a second aperitif, equanimity was gradually restored. Ghosts, he had always believed, came from within oneself and could have no objective existence. Malevolent revenants were the stuff of folklore.

Nevertheless, he could not quite get away from the uneasy feeling that he had inadvertently revealed himself to the unknown, even made an absurd commitment. The portent of those impassioned words spoken in the tomb echoed in his memory and the recollection of their intensity in the face of a buried sexual perversion exhumed by the glass-bound spectre of the beauteous Marietta was indeed pathetic – like falling in love with a statue or a portrait, the stuff of myth and romantic novels. He resolved that while his two encounters with Tall Hat had the makings of a plausible after-dinner story his involuntary proposition to an embalmed corpse was hardly an item for the delectation of prurient colleagues.

He ordered a bottle of *vino rossi* and stayed until nearly eight when he felt ready for *risotto alla Siciliani* at his hotel. Taking out his wallet to pay the bill, he found the drawing of Marietta. He eagerly studied its contours and poured out the remains of the wine. At least she was real, and he had the film in his camera to prove that his memorable encounter with GB's evil art was no figment of an overheated brain.

Well fortified, Crest, a species of Englishman abroad who walks everywhere and summons taxis only as a last resort set out along the darkening streets keeping a wary eye open for the footpads he knew preyed on lone tourists in Palermo. Somewhere along the way he passed a lurker in a doorway who sought to arrest his attention with an obscene gesture. Crest increased his pace, telling himself that in Sicily everyone over fifty wore a hat of some sort.

By now the natural light had yielded to the shadows in the labyrinth of dingy side-streets radiating from the *Corso Calatafimi* and Crest began to realise that he had somehow lost his bearings, for although he had been walking for some time in what he was certain was the right eastwards direction, he seemed to be getting no nearer home. Moreover, it struck him that the broad expanse of cobblestones on which he suddenly found himself, bore a strong resemblance to the *Piazza Cappuccini.* These Italian squares are all much the same at night, he decided, and looked around for a helpful street-sign. When he found one he realised with a grim sense of foreboding that somehow he really had managed to retrace his steps to the area around the *Convento,* now dark and empty of people, and blamed it on his wine-inspired navigation.

But it was not quite empty. A couple stood on the corner; an elderly man and a youngish woman. He'd ask them where he could get a bus or a taxi.

"*Scusi Senor,*" he began. "*Dov'e...?* and exclaimed in disgust, for from the man came a pungent odour. His sunken cheeks, shadowed by that now familiar tall hat, were pitted, his teeth projected and he showed more nostrils than nose. Yet although Crest now understood what the nature of that odour must be, his initial revulsion faded and when the woman, thinly-shrouded, the fleshy contours of her body scarcely concealed, glided forward and silently reached out for him, he felt a strange yet familiar longing. His lips formed the name, "Marietta" as her arms opened to encircle him, but on the very rim of fulfilment he recognised that this was no amorous embrace from his own vital world. An inner voice proclaimed to Crest that if he surrendered he would be drawn helplessly and irrevocably beyond the barrier that secures the quick from the dead, a victim of *il bacio del morte*, the dream kiss, the persistent lover's reward for his grave-defying devotion.

In the safety of daylight Crest might have kept a cooler head and not abandoned himself so quickly to such wild flights of the imagination, but here in the dark *Piazza*, stalked by apparitions, his own medical history, earlier disquiet and the effects of alcohol on an empty stomach, dictated his reactions, further driven by absolute terror of the unknown and the fundamental human instinct for self-preservation. With a supreme effort, Crest tore himself away and ran screaming into a passing *Caribinieri* patrol.

Satisfied that this terrified foreign tourist was neither incapably drunk nor certifiably deranged the *tenente* in charge summoned up sufficient English to observe ambiguously that "human peoples not walking in this very bad place at night". The patrol searched the immediate area but found no such couple as Crest described and as the Englishman was clearly unable to furnish a coherent statement the officers took him to the University Hospital where he was treated for shock. His story, when he was eventually capable of telling it, did not provoke as much surprise as he expected and to his relief was not challenged. Evidently the officers had heard something like it before.

Next day the unfortunate visitor cut his holiday short and returned to London, much lowered in spirit. His departure was not enhanced by the theft of his wallet as he awaited his flight from Palermo's International Airport. The precious sketch went with it. Disappointing, but at least he still had his film. Settled safe at home in West London he had the roll developed, but when he saw the result of the final exposure, bile rose in his throat ... for the picture clearly showed that the transparent coffin with its identifying label housed a shrouded skin-and-bone corpse in that advanced stage of dissolution called in the cryptic jargon of Renaissance art *ein Hautskelett*. It was just recognisable as that of a woman.

There was more. Another cadaver, of a male in somewhat better condition, attired in the ragged remnants of a tail coat, occupied the neighbouring space on the filthy tattered couch. A bony wrist projected from the sleeve of the coat and fleshless fingers appeared to caress the first body in a parody of endearment. A stove-pipe hat had been drawn over the skull and the features were much decayed. Crest was further horrified to see that his photograph revealed, reflected in the glass, the blurred shadow of a man wearing what looked like identical headgear. He could not bring himself to examine the ghastly scene further and in a spasm of fury, triggered by a renewal of his abhorrence, tore up the photograph and burned the negative, actions which he later regretted.

A *post scriptum* is surely in order. A sceptical friend, to whom Crest eventually related a sanitized version, passed unkind remarks about "male menopause", explained the reflected shadow as a flaw in processing and the entire experience as the result of self-hypnosis. Nevertheless this man was curious enough to make enquiries at the Tourist Office in Palermo while passing through the city on a coach holiday a year later. He had no time, he told Crest, to visit the *Convento* and see for himself, but managed to learn from an old Sicilian official that the entrance to the recess which Crest claimed to have entered had been bricked up long before the Second World War on Mussolini's orders after numerous complaints by foreign visitors.

Still more disquieting for poor Crest was the other half of the Sicilian's story, dragged out by judicious bribery. Local legend held that a certain Giancarlo Baroni, sometime a prosperous undertaker in Palermo, had taken the secret of his renowned embalming fluid to the grave or rather to the *Catacombe Cappuccini* where his influential family had contrived to have the body entombed in that same vault, joining his long dead mistress, the infamous harlot Marietta d'Asconi, as recently as 1921.

7. The Boggart of Ruach

I first heard of the Boggart of Ruach from a book posthumously published in 1939 by a Professor Dahlberg, an American folklorist. Ruach is the ancient title of a conical mound on Anglesey, the green land over the Menai Straits known to the Romans as Mona and by later inhabitants as Ynys Mon or Mam Cymru, the Mother Isle of Wales. The erudite Professor suggested in his opening chapter that Ruach may have been a late corruption of the Welsh *crug* or even early Irish *cruachan* = "mountain" though the reality was no mountain, just a bit of a rocky hillock a few hundred feet high in a mainly flat landscape eroded by time, a relic of Anglesey's pre-Cambrian history when a mountain chain did exist.

In the second year of my archaeology studies at Cambridge I became interested in pre-Druidic burial chambers. Examples existed on Anglesey but I'd never heard of Ruach until Dahlberg referred to it as the site of a Druid burial-ground. The Druids had been prominent there until the first century AD when the Roman Suetonius Paulinus and his successor Gaius Agricola unkindly massacred them. Druids had gathered an evil reputation for ritual sacrifice which, though probably unjustified, persisted for centuries.

Unlike other burial places on Anglesey Ruach seemed to have been forgotten. The legend of Ruach's boggart had long engrossed Professor Dahlberg, The traditional image he conjured up associated the Celtic "noonday devil", a carnivorous entity said to pounce on innocent mortals during the heat of high summer, with a type of the Norwegian troll, originally a flesh-devouring creature dwelling in a chilly mountain cave.

Dahlberg implied that this horrific vision was not the fictitious by-product of a myth but a reality.

The Boggart of Ruach, a localised demon with precedents in East European folklore, was a far more terrifying entity than the domestic hobgoblin of that name known in late mediaeval Lancashire and Yorkshire.

Authentic flesh-eating humans had certainly existed. Sawney Bean and his large family of cannibals had lived on the West coast of Galloway towards the end of the sixteenth century and spawned a legend of immortal ghouls. According to Professor Dahlberg the word obviously derived from the same root as *bogey* and the older *bogle* which had currency in Scotland about the same time.

Dahlberg argued that the Islamic threat of abduction by a ghoul had merged with the pagan Celtic belief in the sinister power of caves to enchant. Though most Welsh myths concerned kindly faery spirits, linked with rivers, streams and mountains and having human characteristics, when they chose to lure mortals into their "otherworld" retreats their purpose was to dance and feast, but the Ruach boggart was a denizen of a different kind, hostile to intruders. Dahlberg traced its origin to tales of phantoms believed to guard burial chambers in central Turkey.

At first I dismissed Dahlberg's volume as unselective and unscholarly, relying too much on hearsay and anecdotal evidence. One of the Professor's numerous footnotes stated that there was a cave somewhere on Ruach, which in accordance with pagan Celtic lore, could be entered only by faery invitation or by unfortunate accident; unfortunate because to find it would arouse the Boggart. In the mind of an enthusiast fed by local gossip, any mean hollow in the earth might be the entrance to an "otherworld" realm ruled not by beneficent faeries but by a merciless tyrant who emerged on occasion to feed on the unwary.

From my limited undergraduate experience in field-work I had learned that the foundation of such stories was rarely as ancient as the tellers claimed. Most of the more intriguing details, such as the witch's warning, sudden shape-changing or a fatal recognition scene, originating in Greek myth and implying a direct threat to the living, were invented by local authors owning the bardic gift of colourful narrative. The Professor included one gem of this kind when he warned his readers that this malevolent spectre sometimes disguised itself to look "like someone you knew already". To meet the Ruach boggart in whatever shape meant forcible removal to a deep subterranean cavern where this apparition had its lair.

An old wives' tale I decided, presented as fact in a manner unworthy of a serious scholar, but a yellowed cutting from a national newspaper pasted to the endpaper of the library copy made me slightly less sceptical. The extract noted the strange disappearance in Anglesey of Professor Irvin Dahlberg, PhD, aged 54, of Eastern University in Florida. The Professor, described as a well-known authority on pagan survivals, had lectured to local groups on unexplained abductions in the area which he attributed to supernatural forces. The report referred to the missing man's conviction that the old myth of a predatory monster, known locally as the Boggart, was directly based on fact. Police investigations were continuing. The Bangor coroner returned an open verdict while pointing out the dangers of exploring archaeological sites alone. He recommended that cautionary notices be placed in an appropriate place. Somebody had appended the words: *never seen again so cherchez la femme boggart not rubbish.* The cryptic comment provided a disquieting reminder of the strength of regional superstition.

But was there anything in it? I resolved to find out. Absorbing the heritage of North Wales had to wait for my attention since after my nervous breakdown, due to overwork, I finished my degree with a disappointing result and was handed call-up papers for two years military service. I forgot about Dahlberg and the riddle of his abrupt departure from human ken.

I might never have thought about him again had not the Army posted me to a holding battalion outside Bangor, to await a War Office Selection Board and marking time under instruction on a motor-cycling course. Eight "potential officers" quartered in Morton Barracks were learning to ride a standard Matchless. We used to sally forth in convoy and chug up and down the country roads for a couple of hours four mornings a week. The exercise was great fun with little risk of accident as we were held down to a speed-limit of 15 mph. Our Selection Boards had been delayed and we expected to be there for at least another seven weeks.

I didn't mind. My interest in Welsh legends had flagged since the Army took over my life but now some of the old enthusiasm returned. The opportunity to explore a hidden tract of romantic Anglesey was not to be missed. Moreover, the name of Dahlberg was prominent in an article by a local journalist bearing the arresting caption DID THE PROFESSOR MEET THE BOGGART? His contribution was one of a series on local mysteries.

This writer, one Ted Edwards, had rehashed, with acknowledgement, parts of an old book called *Early History of Mona* by Evan Partridge, Partridge, a Victorian parson and popular local historian, claimed that "scores of people" had disappeared from the Druidic mound of Ruach through the centuries, taken by a deadly monster known as the Boggart to an underground cavern where they were torn to pieces and devoured. Edwards recalled the fate, fifteen years earlier, of "the distinguished American author Professor Irwin Dahlberg, a man tragically obsessed with the legend that had grown up around the mountain" and outlined what was known about Dahlberg's last day, when he was seen in the company of a woman high on the north slope in the late afternoon of July 22nd 1938, having announced in the course of a talk to the local archaeological society that he had identified the entrance to a Neolithic burial chamber.

The scrawl on the press-cutting had implied the presence of a woman. This was at first thought to be Dahlberg's sister, who had travelled from the United States to visit him, but it turned out that she was in London at the time. Edwards cited Dahlberg's disquieting story of the boggart and its shape-shifting capacity to look "like someone you knew already", winding up with a lurid warning to anyone foolish enough to climb the Hill of Ruach when "the monster" might be abroad, seeking the flesh of yet another over-confident intruder hoping to expose its hideout. He supported those public-spirited persons who had long-insisted that only a thorough excavation of the mound by an experienced team using modern techniques could determine if such a chamber existed and regretted that local reservation societies had so far resisted proposals to employ mechanical diggers.

After three weeks we were presumed to be expert enough on our steeds to venture on a longer exercise and the corporal-instructor despatched us on a run across the Menai Bridge to Beaumaris. In single file we crossed the narrow Straits with the naval training ship HMS Conway at anchor below and trailed our bored leader along the unspoilt coastline.

An invigorating drive along the coastal road brought us to Beaumaris, now a popular marina for holidaymakers but then noted in the guide-books for its late 13th-century castle, erected by Edward I to keep the Welsh chieftains in check. I didn't get a chance to see this formidable pile close-up but the corporal-instructor gave us time off for a lengthy tea-break. We parked opposite the public library and on impulse I went in. The librarian was an elderly man wearing thick, pebble lenses and a patched sports jacket. Pinned to the lapel was a card identifying him as "Walford Williams, BA".

I asked him if he knew of a hill named Ruach on Anglesey, supposed to be haunted,

"Ruach?" he queried. "That's an old name, bach. Druid burials. Haunted? Who knows? You'll have been reading Ted's bit in the paper. Sensational stuff. But I'd be careful up there man. It was a battle-school at the start of the war. The Army closed it down in 1940. I'm told the barbed wire's still there. I've never been up myself".

When I mentioned my own bachelor's degree Mr Williams, sensing a kindred spirit, launched into an account of an old Welsh romance about a savage serpent that lived on the Dolorous Mound or Mountain. Mortals did well to steer clear of mounds, he informed me lugubriously and especially of the north slope. North slopes were reserved as burial-places for evildoers. Realising that my interest was serious he indicated the unholy spot marked on a pre-war Ordnance Survey, some distance from a hamlet called Cwm Beris. The Holyhead bus would take me so far but after Cwm Beris I'd have to walk about a mile through a wood to the mound.

"The wood's still called Boggart Forest". Do you know Partridge's *Early History of Mona*? That's where Ted Edwards got most of his stuff".

Yes, I had heard of it. He searched his archives and dug out a leather-bound volume "partly translated from the Welsh by the late Reverend Evan Partridge BD, Holyhead MDCCCLXV", indicating a section where the author had inserted a reference to cave-hunters "taken by the Devil" from the north face of the mound. It was not clear whether he meant the theological Devil or the noonday one.

The Ordnance Survey did not refer to Ruach by name. Local guide-books concentrated on Beaumaris Castle and mentioned "various sites of archaeological interest" but no Ruach. I bought a handy road map from a newsagent and found Cwm Beris but Ruach was not named on this one either though cartographical signs for a bushy-topped hill indicated where it must lie.

My fellow-trainees were ready to start on the road back so I had no time to study old Partridge further. Like Ted Edwards, Professor Dahlberg must have used Partridge, itself a partial translation, as a primary source including his warning that the infamous boggart would make its approach in familiar form. I didn't recall seeing a reference to Partridge in Dahlberg's bibliography nor could the helpful Mr Williams identify the Welsh original, if indeed there had ever been one.

A couple of weeks after I first arrived at Morton Barracks I had been none too happy to renew my acquaintance with a fellow named Pat Brightman whom I had known at school. He was a burly rugger-playing type, a natural bully and I had been his natural target, one of several who had suffered at his hands, Even then he had been a determined chaser of girls – "skirt" as he called them. I was not happy to see him and was dismayed to find that he had not changed. He had already got himself promoted to Temporary Acting Lance-Corporal and put in charge of our Hut 37.

Our paths were to cross in another way. I met a girl in Bangor, a student at a Teachers Training College. Her name was Bryony Rees. Love flourished briefly until I made the fatal mistake of introducing her to the other chaps, Brightman included, at an "Other Ranks" dance.

He got off his mark right away and commandeered her. "Frailty thy name is Bryony, eh, Slimy?" was what he said to me a few days afterwards. 'Slimy' was what he called me at school but I didn't think he'd he have the gall to use it in front of her. No doubt he told her some lie about why I got that name. It was really just an unpleasant schoolboy corruption of my surname, Sloman.

Brightman soon stamped out the flame of my budding romance. At the next dance she was on his arm when he winked and treated me to another of his smart asides.

"Faint heart never won fair lady, Slimy old boy".

I was left in no doubt as to the nature of their relationship. To him she was just another "bit of skirt".

With no other distraction to occupy me my attention returned to Ruach. One of our tests as leaders of men was to give a ten-minute talk on a subject of our own choosing. I held forth about Ted's article, Dahlberg's book, Partridge's boggart and the grisly fate of those who had set out to find the cave. Brightman barged in and said he'd done a lot of potholing in Galway and invited himself to lead a Ruach expedition. Weekends were always a problem as there were few attractions outside the barracks apart from the cinema or the pub, although Brightman had now found another, as he frequently reminded me over the following three weeks.

His unwelcome proposal therefore came as a surprise. He proposed we all go to Ruach on our bikes. He'd arrange things with the corporal-instructor. None of the others wanted to waste their precious Saturday on a caving expedition so that left me. After my talk I could hardly back out though Brightman was the last man I'd have chosen as a companion. He could only get one bike but it didn't matter as he said he would drive and I could ride pillion.

Saturday's weather was changeable and rain was predicted. He resolved to chance it and by two p.m. we were on our way. The sight of helmeted trainee soldiers on motor cycles was common and provided we weren't stopped by inquisitive Redcaps and kept our speed down, we should be there and back by supper-time.

Once over the Bridge, we covered the seven miles to Beaumaris without incident and consulted my map. A road in the south-western direction branched off from the main bus route to Holyhead and led to a low-lying stretch with cornfields on either side. Our earlier confidence waned when the blue sky suddenly blackened over and it started to rain heavily. We hadn't brought our capes and soon got wet. Pools of water spread across the track, turning the dirt surface into a morass.

The last leg was rougher than expected. The secondary road hadn't seen repair for years and it took us the best part of an hour weaving around the potholes to reach Cwm Beris, a no-place made up of a few scattered cottages, a chapel and a vandalized phone-box. Where the track shrank into a footpath we left our mud-spattered mount propped up against a hollow oak tree and made slow progress on an upward slope through gradually thickening undergrowth and mist rising from the damp ground. The path took us into a copse and then ran out altogther. I realised that this must be "Boggart Forest", an example of the native capacity for exaggeration.

By this time I was soaking and my body had lost heat. Lance-Corporal Brightman forged ahead, heedless of the overhanging branches and the vicious stinging nettles, needle-sharp enough to penetrate our serge trousers. I was not nearly so impervious to these irritating obstacles and had my self-styled leader been less persuasive I might have given up.

"Come on Slimy old man, you'll never make an officer. What's the matter with you! Get a move on!"

I spotted a wooden notice in faded red paint attached to a tree with rusty nails and decorated with a crude skull-and-crossbones:

WAR DEPARTMENT
DANGER
KEEP OUT

That must be a relic of the wartime training-ground. A little farther on, we came upon another, somewhat more conciliatory, but just as alarming:

ANCIENT BURIAL SITE
VISITORS ARE ADVISED NOT TO
PROCEED ALONE BEYOND THIS POINT

One reason for these discouraging warnings immediately became clear. The way was barred by a wide stretch of boggy ground. Planks had been thrown across it to help visitors, "preferably proceeding alone" to get to the other side. Brightman laughed and made some comment about falling in and drowning. I said nothing. I knew something about the properties of certain bogs. That's where the Druid priests were said to bury their torture victims. A body sucked down rarely came up again. Tollund Man in Denmark was a rare exception. He'd been strangled, probably as part of a sacrifice. The peat had preserved him for thousands of years and left his features recognisably human.

We stepped over the planks very carefully without looking down. Then, all at once, the mass of rain-soaked vegetation cleared and the Mound of Ruach reared up before us. After all I'd read and heard the first sight of this fabled peak was disappointing. It was neither very steep, nor very high – just a grassy hump of a few hundred feet, overgrown with nettles and rising gradually to an irregular summit with scraggy bushes dotted about on the ridge. The uneven surface was pitted with rabbit-holes and shallow trenches partly filled with water.

We stood for a moment contemplating the scene. "Phew", I said, "Not much to write home about. Not a soul in sight and no wonder".

"Oh, I dunno," he answered, shading his eyes and squinting. The rain had stopped and the there was a faint rainbow in the sky but this place could never be other than grim. Why on earth had I come here and with Brightman of all people?

My companion pointed upwards. "We're not alone. There's somebody up there, right at the top, a chap in uniform looking at us; must be from the barracks".

He was rated a "marksman" by the Army and his eyesight must have been better than mine. I could see nobody.

"Come on. Let's go and scout round," he said," I've got a flashlight. Maybe we'll find this cave of yours".

He filled his pipe from a leather tobacco pouch and lit it.

"Look at this pouch Slimy old man. My initials. Monogrammed. A Happy Birthday Present for Acting Lance-Corporal Brightman. Bryony gave me that? Did you know we're engaged? Unofficially of course". He winked. "Thanks for introducing us. No hard feelings. OK?"

I had hard feelings all right but I kept them to myself. This lout had a hide like a rhino. Did he have any idea of how I had felt about Bryony? She was just a pick-up for him but for me it had been serious. I felt one of my migraines coming on.

"I wish you'd stop calling me Slimy", I said. "My name's Adrian".

"OK Slimy ... I mean Adrian" was his rejoinder. "Adrian it is." He buttoned the pouch into the pocket of his well-cut battledress and started up the slope, trailing smoke.

The day was not going to improve. I didn't enjoy Brightman's company nor was I comfortable on Ruach now that I was actually there. The place had a strange cloying atmosphere, nauseating and – I hesitate to say – evil. I could well believe in the hidden presence of an ill-disposed underworld, even in daylight. My desire to know more about Ruach melted away. A quick survey would be enough … then back to the boring, comfortable security of the barracks.

Brightman ascended the face of the mound alone, trailing smoke from his pipe and holding his flashlight while I sat down on a rock and watched his back receding. He was clearly very fit and in a short time would have reached the ridge. Half-way up the slope he turned and yelled excitedly.

"Look here! I've found a gap that could be a cave. Come on man!"

Reluctantly I dragged myself up that slope. The last downpour had transformed the surface into a marsh. I slipped on the grass and fell heavily. Then I banged my head on a rock and went down again. When I picked myself up I had lost sight of Brightman but in a few moments I had reached the place where he had been standing.

My brave companion had indeed stumbled on a black hole obscured by weeds and just wide enough to let a man squeeze through. I peered into the hole and could just make out what looked like rough steps. The pale light from his flashlight provided scant illumination. Nothing on earth would have persuaded me to go down there.

I needn't have worried. Brightman had to live up to his claim as an experienced caver and pushed me aside.

"I want to see what's down there. Might be the cave those writers of yours were on about".

"It's just a hole," I said, "and not very deep. Runs along just below the surface."

"You stay here and keep a look out. The steps must lead somewhere," he insisted. "I saw something like it in Somerset".

He knocked out his pipe and wriggled into the aperture, whistling cheerfully. Almost immediately he called back. "It widens once you're in. It's a proper cave all right. Goes in a long way by the look of it. There's nearly room to stand up."

I lit a cigarette and waited near the mouth of the cave for him to reappear. After a few minutes I yelled out his name. Not a sound. No answer. He'd had an accident, fallen into a pit, broken a leg – all sorts of explanations flashed through my mind. I now had a throbbing headache.

Then I noticed something that made me catch my breath. Were my eyes deceiving me or had the entrance got smaller? Was it shrinking? No, that couldn't be. But it was. No longer could a man of normal girth get in.

Nor get out! My heart jumped. If he didn't hurry, Brightman would be hopelessly trapped. I bent down and shouted at him to come out. Already too late. I watched helplessly as the opening lost its roughly circular shape and visibly contracted.

A rational portion of my brain told me that this couldn't be happening. The surface earth had subsided, bringing the roof of the tunnel down and causing on a smaller scale the crushing disaster that happened in coal mines. The dangers associated with this treacherous hill were brought about by natural not supernatural forces. The boggart *was* rubbish. On the other hand, the cave mouth was diminishing even as I stood there. Brightman would be buried alive!

But what could I do? Find someone. Get help, spades to dig up the ground. Perhaps Brightman was not completely buried, just trapped by the fall with enough air to last a few hours. That chap on the ridge. Where was he? The hole had almost gone. Now a rabbit could hardly have got through it.

I shaded my eyes and saw that relief was at hand. The man in uniform on the ridge had already begun to descend. He must have seen that something was wrong. My shouts died inside the cave mouth. All I got was an echo of my own voice. I shouted again and this time sensed a presence right behind me and spun round. There was a soldier standing there. One stripe. My first reaction was relief, for it was Pat Brightman himself. Somehow he had found another way out. But how could he have come up behind me? I looked for the soldier coming down from the ridge but could see no sign of him. There was only Brightman, but his attitude made me uneasy.

"Brightman, what happened to you, are you all right?"

He didn't look all right. Far from it. He glowered at me with a strange animal light in his eyes as if he'd never seen me before. His normal healthy colour had been sucked out and his familiar features seemed to be melting, eyes and nose blending into a stark white face like a clown's mask. His mouth gaped wolfishly, exposing projecting teeth. He'd gone mad down in the cave. Something down in the cave had changed him, like…

And that's when the penny dropped. *Like someone you knew already.* Wasn't that what Partridge and Dahlberg had claimed? Here lay proof. This dreadful ogre from another dimension, the so-called boggart, was solid. Where the real Pat Brightman was didn't bear thinking about.

"You're … not him!" I screamed. "Get away from me! Don't touch me.

He, or it … the thing with the fading remnants of Brightman's face was going to attack me. I looked around for a weapon but all I could find was a half-brick. I hurled it as hard as I could and caught the false creature on its misshapen head. It squealed. It could be hurt.

Then I ran for my life. Fear lashed my stiffened limbs into action. Blindly I stumbled down the hill, tripping over rocks and into the 'Boggart Forest'. It was well-named.

I heard shuffling noises behind me. Barbed wire lacerated my legs and arms but I felt no pain. I can't remember how I got back to where we had left the Matchless and found myself alone, too weak to sit on the saddle. That vicious migraine headache came back and made me feel sick but eventually I got the machine started and wobbled back to Cwm Beris.

I didn't stop to telephone. The rest of the journey along the coast road from Beaumaris was a blank.

Crossing the Bridge to the mainland my head cleared and I began to see how this tragedy might be regarded in a light unfavourable to me. I had no witnesses. Pat Brightman had been buried alive and I'd seen the boggart, a deceiving demon who looked like him.

That sounded crazy even to me. Would they believe it? The Army wouldn't praise me for deserting a comrade in distress because I'd seen a … whatever it was. They'd deliver me to the headshrinkers. I'd suffered plenty of those at Cambridge. This was a no-win situation.

I pulled up at a workmen's cafe and asked for some tea while I thought it over. In the end I made up my mind to tell the absolute truth 'without fear or favour', as they say. It didn't occur to me at that stage that I might be made to face something far more intimidating than a Medical Board.

My troubles began right away.

"Been in an accident mate?" someone asked. A Redcap. He'd spotted the Matchless parked outside. I must have looked a mess. He took my name and number and escorted me back to the barracks. The guard commander regarded my dishevelled state and telephoned the duty officer. He listened to my explanation incredulously and called out Camp Security, a Captain Fowler and a bleary-eyed Sergeant-major. The latter hastily organized an emergency rescue team with picks and shovels and ordered me to show them where I'd last seen Lance-Corporal Brightman.

So far they weren't unsympathetic. My return journey in a Dodge truck took less than half the time we'd spent on the bike. Captain Fowler followed in his Jeep. By now the daylight was fading. The vehicles were parked where we had left the Matchless. Two medical squaddies carried a stretcher through the wood and up the hill but, as I expected, the mound was deserted. Of Pat Brightman or his ferocious simulacrum, no visible trace remained and although the team dug out the area where the cave had been to a depth of six feet, the earth was solid. There was no sign, either of recent subsidence or of a hollow leading to a cave. The earth on all sides of the slope where I had met the monster was undisturbed. An eagle-eyed squaddie spotted Brightman's pipe at the bottom of the incline.

I simply couldn't understand it. Neither could the rescuers.

Fowler ordered a search for a recently-dug grave. That gave me some indication as to how the wind was blowing. Not favourably. He drove off to Cwm Beris to call the nearest police-station. Why hadn't I done that, he asked. I didn't tell him the 'phone box was out of order.

No stone was left unturned, literally. When it got too dark to see by natural light they circled the mound with powerful torches, cursing the barbed wire and the man responsible for ruining their Saturday night, namely myself. The occupants of Hut 37 were not popular with the permanent camp staff.

Captain Fowler's call produced two suspicious policemen who gave me fishy looks and said I'd have to make a statement. The Sergeant-major announced in graphic terms that he didn't believe a single blankety word I'd said. No-one spoke to me on the return trip.

Back at Morton Barracks Captain Fowler told me I was under close arrest pending further investigations. I spent a slumber-free night in the guard-room. The search for Acting Lance-Corporal Brightman continued without me and without success.

Next day the police, led by a balding Chief-Inspector named George Bastian, turned it into a murder case with me as prime suspect though they couldn't establish a plausible motive and had no material evidence, such as a body, on which to base even a preliminary charge. With obvious relief Fowler handed me over "to help with enquiries".

On reading my signed statement Chief-Inspector Bastian scratched the back of his head. "Well Mr Sloman, he said with a genial grin, "I must congratulate you on your gift for writing fiction. In all my years on the Force I've never heard anything like it".

I asked for a lawyer and he said one was on his way, a Mr Aylward. In the meantime he did his best to get me to confess. His tone varied from friendly to wheedling. "Now son, off the record, we know you killed him. What we don't know is why, or how. Come on, you're an intelligent man, got a degree, going to be an officer weren't you? We're not stupid either. Surely you don't expect us to swallow that yarn? Ghosts, ghouls? Holes that shrink? Underground caves? Not to mention our boggart? Try and see it our way son. Make it easy on yourself and tell us the truth. Save us all a lot of trouble. Just say where you buried the lad's body and we'll put in a good word for you".

After half an hour of Bastian's velvet-fist version of the third degree, Mr Aylward arrived, an old boy with a Devon accent who warned me of the weight that circumstantial evidence might carry against my tale of the boggart, which frankly he found quite incredible. I was beginning to find it incredible myself.

A sympathetic female psychologist asked me if I'd mind taking an IQ test. "No thanks," I told her. I'd had one of those from the shrinks in Cambridge. I'd scored 142 on that, the sort of score which people with good Honours degrees make. "How did you do in your finals?" she asked innocently.

None of her business, but I saw no reason to conceal the fact that I'd cracked up and been awarded an *aegrotat*, an unclassified degree given out of grace and favour to chaps who weren't fit to sit finals. That might have been a mistake. It had nothing to do with this case. Policemen like Bastian were prone to connect nervous breakdown with borderline insanity and jump to misleading conclusions.

I asked the Chief-Inspector if he had taken the trouble to look for the other chap in Army uniform, surely equally suspect.

"Oh yes we have," he grinned, "but he hasn't come forward. Perhaps the ghoul ate him up!"

They all laughed at his dazzling wit and I joined in, but they didn't get me to change my story. How could I? It was absolute fact as far as I was concerned.

Bastian rattled on about "brainstorms" and loss of memory.

"Sooner or later we'll find that body," he told me confidently, "and it'll go down better with a jury at the trial if you tell me where it is now."

When I replied that the boggart had taken Brightman down to its lair, he threw up his hands in mock despair. A detective asked a police artist to draw the boggart to my directions and when he saw the result suggested I plead insanity if I didn't want to be hanged.

That did scare me. I hadn't thought of a trial, far less its possible consequences.

In spite of these clumsy scare tactics I was released from police custody without charge and returned to the Army's care. So far as that organization was concerned, I was far from stainless. Captain Fowler informed me that my Selection Board had been cancelled *pro-tem* and immediate posting to another holding battalion in South Wales confirmed. That night I was put on a train under escort. Chief-Inspector Bastian saw me off.

The case sold papers. Ted Edwards earned himself an instant reputation as a fearless investigative reporter outside the length and breadth of Snowdonia. His reports were widely syndicated and though I never met him in person I was to have good reason to be grateful to Ted. He was nothing if not thorough. His detailed account of the dangers of Ruach and its murky history of inexplicable disappearances even involved trainee soldiers early in the war. He had even got hold of the police artist's drawing of the boggart which was published in all the national papers. His articles, quoting extensively from Partridge and Dahlberg, must have weighed in favour of the boggart's existence. Remaindered copies of Dahlberg's book were much in demand and Partridge's *Early History of Mona* was hurriedly reprinted.

After two months in a camp near Swansea I was brought back to Bangor to be chief witness at the coroner's inquest, held, unusually, in camera, when I was able to repeat my story on oath. Walford Williams described my visit to his library. A mining engineer rambled on about subsidence. The Army in the person of Captain Fowler described its part in the search and gave me a good character. They could hardly do less for a "potential officer". My beloved Bryony described me as an old friend who had introduced her to Patrick. No they weren't really engaged. On that afternoon she had been to the cinema with her real fiancé, a young man named Hargreaves. Chief-Inspector Bastian's evidence was fair to me though he made my repeated statement about the shape-changing boggart sound ridiculous, which of course it was not.

My previous medical history was never mentioned. I suppose they weren't allowed to do that in court or maybe the lady psychologist did suppress it. It might have embarrassed the Army to have to explain how I'd been passed fit for service, but then, after all, I was just a witness, not the accused, and without a *corpus delicti* the circumstantial evidence was thin.

The case never went to trial. How could it? The jury returned an open verdict, just as in the case of Professor Dahlberg fifteen years before. Although the court's verdict forced the Army to accept my story, after several interviews a trio of Army doctors recommended my discharge "without prejudice", conditional upon entering a psychiatric hospital for the remainder of my term of service. They said I suffered from "dangerous delusions". I didn't mind. My chance of further promotion had gone and I didn't fancy eighteen months of spud-bashing.

On my solemn oath I had told the court the whole truth and nothing but the truth about what happened that July afternoon and my conscience remains clear. Even so, a sceptical element in the Army and the frustrated Chief-Inspector Bastian preferred to believe the worst. Brightman senior threatened to bring a private prosecution but never did.

They sent me to a comfortable place outside Edinburgh and I was able to get on with some serious academic work. I thought I'd heard the last of Ruach, but in 1960 the municipal authorities, after years of pressure from the police, consented to have the north slope of the "notorious mountain" uncovered. By that time I was a postgraduate student preparing a doctoral dissertation on the modern preservation of ancient Celtic beliefs in Scotland, another tangled skein to unravel.

Ted Edwards triumphantly reported the preliminary result of an excavation in the national press under the headline 'CHARNEL HOUSE MYSTERY', announcing that:

"careful digging to fifty feet underground had exposed a chamber carved out of the earth in which half-chewed human bones were scattered, together with remnants of clothing. A narrow tunnel leading to a hollow near the surface may have provided entrance and exit for some savage creature whose nature must surely baffle the modern imagination."

At first I was delighted to have apologists for the old Ruach legend vindicated, but I felt very sad when I read a separate account on an inside page, not by Ted, of the discovery by foresters of a well-preserved body floating on the surface of a deep bog in a wood known locally as Boggart's Forest. It was headed:

'TRAGIC FIND AFTER EARTH TREMOR. QUAGMIRE GIVES UP ITS DEAD'.

My old inquisitor George Bastian, now a Superintendent, had issued a statement. A pathologist described the remains as those of a male in his twenties which had been concealed for at least five years until a recent seismic shock had raised it to the surface. Death had been caused by an injury to the skull consistent with a blow by a blunt object. Fragments of a bloodstained Army uniform together with a leather tobacco pouch inscribed with the monogrammed initials P.B. and a pocket flashlight were found with the corpse, discoveries which suggest that a former police investigation might now be re-opened. A Mrs Briony Withenshaw, formerly Rees, has come forward with important evidence.

"*Cherchez la femme* and ye shall find", I thought ruefully.

Eager reporters with long memories soon invaded my ivory-tower privacy. Naturally I had nothing new to say though I left them mulling over the interesting proposition that a few of those half-chewed bones probably belonged to Professor Dahlberg deceived by the boggart in the form of his sister.

8. *A Railway Child*

Before the Second World War, I used to travel every summer from London to the North of Scotland to stay with maternal grandparents in Kinlonie, a village fifteen miles inland from Aberdeen. On that sunny day in August 1939, Father, a widower and a regular officer in the Sappers, saw me off. This was the very first year that I'd been trusted to travel all that distance by myself; thanks to Hitler he couldn't get away from the War Office.

The Flying Scotsman pulled out of King's Cross punctually at ten a.m. I didn't have time to visit the footplate of the powerful green 4-6-2 'Pacific' at the head of the train, but I remember its nameplate, *Blinkbonny*. Snug in my corner seat I surrendered to the heady excitement of the non-stop journey to Edinburgh, gathering speed northwards through Grantham, Peterborough and York to my beloved Scotland. Crossing the Border Bridge at Berwick always fired my imagination with childish but intense national pride. I had a momentary glimpse of the castle high up on the rock before the express glided gently to a stop under the roof of Waverly Station, where the engine was changed and after a short delay, a less aristocratic steed than *Blinkbonny* hauled the surviving coaches over those magnificent Forth and Tay bridges to Dundee, Arbroath and beyond, grinding to a final halt at the joint terminus in the Granite City of Aberdeen, where I was born. What excitement for a twelve-year-old!

This was as far North as the remains of the London express penetrated. Passengers desiring to venture further crossed the concourse and boarded the seven o'clock express to Elgin and

Speyside. I congratulated myself on having got this far without adult assistance and proudly showed my first-class ("child's") ticket like a seasoned traveller.

To get to Monymuir passengers had to change trains at the Royal Burgh of Kinlonie. The branch to Monymuir had a single track, and the little train stopped at two intermediate stations before terminating at Monymuir. After so many annual holidays, this had all become familiar territory to me.

The Monymuir-bound train consisted of two carriages, un-coupled from the main-line train and drawn by a once green vintage 0-6-0 workhorse with a high smoke-stack, built in Old-meldrum in 1868. She bore the name *Meldrum Meggie* on a brass plate and the letters *GNSR* in gold on her tender, signifying that she was a relic of the old Great North of Scotland Railway.

That blackened old engine and her ancient crew were bosom friends of mine. Her driver was named Donald and his fireman Andy. They weren't really ancient, just vintage. Donald was close to retirement, myopic and colour-blind. He relied on Andy to tell him whether a yellow "distant" signal was in the up or the down position and whether "Cushnie" the skeletal guard was waving a green flag to send the train on its way or a red one to order it to stand still. They made a perfect team and for years had managed to shield Donald's affliction from the attentions of the area management.

Granddad was a brusque old cavalryman from the Royal Scot-tish Horse, with a chestful of medals from the Great War. His seventeenth-century granite cottage, encircled by a high stone dyke, looked over at Kinlonie Station where *Meldrum Meg*, hissing clouds of steam, used to bring in the train from Mony-muir twice daily and clank to a stop alongside a short platform separated from our dyke by a footpath. A perch on top of the dyke afforded me a privileged view of the railway's comings and goings, from the main line expresses as they thundered past to Speyside, hauled by powerful 4-6-0 B12s, known affectionately as 'Hikers' because of the fat little storage tank carried behind their funnels, to the suburban trains for Keith and Huntly conveyed by less glamorous 4-4-0 D40s, the workhorses of the old North British stable.

For years Donald and Andy had been my faithful summer allies, ever ready to welcome me on to the footplate when Angus Macdonald, the grumpy old stationmaster, wasn't looking and occasionally even let me push the regulator to start Meggie rolling from the coaling-shed to the turntable and watering-point in the shunting-yard. They always made time for me, this little boy from London, a far-off magical city where neither of them had ever been. Donald, a contemplative man, was rarely seen without his pipe. He read a lot, political books mostly, but did not speak much.

Andy made up for his taciturnity. He was a simpler soul who actually believed that Sherlock Holmes was a real living person. I could claim personal memories of Baker Street from visits to Madame Tussaud's and had once lived in Norwood, the scene of one of Holmes's cases, which raised my status in Andy's estimation. I named him "Mister Sherlock Holmes". He always responded with "Doctor Watson" and called Angus MacDonald the grumpy stationmaster "Professor Moriarty", though never to his face.

Those were idyllic summers, but like all earthly versions of paradise, once lost they were unlikely to be regained. In September 1939 the British Expeditionary Force embarked for France. Heavy air-raids on London were expected to start at once so it was decided that I should live in Kinlonie until it was safe to return home. A friend of Father's found me a place as a day-boy in a "suitable" school and so I began to travel the fifteen miles from Kinlonie to Aberdeen, rising at the crack of dawn so as not to miss the main line connection from Keith and Huntly and returning with the evening train.

In that autumn of 1939 the war was not expected to go on far beyond Christmas. At first I was delighted at the prospect of a longer stay in Kinlonie, though childishly disappointed that I might be denied the excitement of seeing air-raids at first-hand, but I soon came to hate my new routine, particularly in the first freezing months of 1940, the worst winter for many years. The Aberdeen school, a grinding, soulless academy, allowed me no time for the former delights of the station-yard and I saw little of *Meldrum Meg* and her keepers, though I heard Donald and Andy shunting her every morning before the main-line train pulled in at ten-to-eight.

By spring the glamour of bygone days spent as a free agent in Kinlonie had faded and I yearned for my London school, but Father, newly promoted to Lieutenant-Colonel, had joined the B.E.F. "somewhere in France" and preferred that his only son should continue to stay under a safe roof well away from possible enemy action and pursue his education without aerial interruption.

The unexpected often happens. After the Germans invaded Norway and Denmark our shipping lanes in the North Sea were open to air attacks from Stavanger and Aalborg and with them harbour towns along the north-east coast of Scotland. Months before any bombs fell on the South of England they were regularly dropped in and around Aberdeen, Fraserburgh, Peterhead and even on inland villages of little or no military importance.

One Saturday morning early in May, while our soldiers were in retreat before Dunkirk, a stick of 250-pounders fell across Kinlonie. I was off school in bed with 'flu' when 'Jerry' dropped his bombs and remember Meggie puffing away in the shunting yard as usual. I didn't actually see the enemy but just on nine o'clock I heard the drone of aircraft, getting louder, then the rattle of machine-guns and several sickening thumps, each nearer than the one before. The last was very close, practically on top of the house. The whole place shook and panes of glass were blown out of my bedroom window. Grandma was in her kitchen, Granddad "digging for victory" in his vegetable garden. He actually spotted the German, a Dornier "Flying Pencil", coming in very low down and trailing black smoke with a Hurricane hard on its tail.

The 'flu' wasn't enough to keep me from the excitement. I sprang out of bed and pulled on some clothes over my pyjamas. Granddad and I went out to find out what had happened. Angus Macdonald the stationmaster and Wullie Rae the local policeman were trying to stop excited people from invading the shunting-yard. Constable Rae informed Grandfather that "a big boom", the last of a stick of four, had landed "somewhere up by the turntable". A horrible sick feeling went right to the pit of my stomach when I remembered that Meggie was usually reversed and watered at about nine. I could so easily have been riding with the old engine, helping Andy to pull her around.

We hurried up the footpath and down the short platform. The air was full of smoke and stench and loud voices came from the direction of the booking-office. My first thoughts were of Donald and Andy and not least, of dear old *Meldrum Meggie*. I prayed that none of them had been hurt. The coaling-shed, a massive concrete structure, had been hit and badly damaged. The first bomb must have gone right through the wooden roof. I left Grandpa and ran to the end of the platform. Beyond the signal-box the tracks leading to the turntable from the shed ended abruptly at a scene of disorder, obscured by a veil of dust.

Ignoring Angus's and Grandpa's angry shouts I ran further, hopping between the rails and dreading what I might find. The turntable was twisted, along with the gantry which supported the watering-point. Apart from that and a gaping bomb crater, damage seemed minimal. Silence hung in the air though *Meldrum Meggie* was letting off steam, with her regulator pump visibly beating and her boiler already turned to face in the direction of Monymuir. Her original dark green livery had been restored to its pristine green colour and her brass bodywork gleamed like the morning sun. I'd never seen her shining like this before. She was really glowing. Normally she got along with the minimum of grooming.

Donald was leaning half out of his cab peering short-sightedly with Andy behind him leaning on his shovel and holding the chain of the thick watering-hose. Donald gestured with his pipe, nodding cheerfully in my direction. Andy was laughing and his lips framed some words which I couldn't make out. So happy was I to see them both safe and sound that I blurted out my old familiar greeting, "Mister Sherlock Holmes I presume?"

This time Andy's expression changed to mock-serious and he pointed behind me. I'm certain that he mouthed two words, not "Doctor Watson" as he usually did but "Professor Moriarty" a second before a voice grated in my ear. I turned sharply to see red-faced Angus Macdonald, in his shirtsleeves and without his uniform jacket and gold-braided cap. He was out of breath and in one of his bullying moods.

"Whit div yuh think ye're up tae? Kin yuh no see it's hellish dangerous? Yon Jerry let go four booms. Could still be anither ane unexploded. Back yuh go. Yer grandfaither's lookin' for yuh".

I could see no signs of danger and this "boom" had certainly gone off but in the station-master's domain it was not wise for me to argue.

Although my Caledonian antecedents were at least as impeccable as his own, Angus took me for "English", a London snob with a "pan loaf" accent who fancied himself a cut above the lads from the village "Higher Grade" school. He didn't realise what a snob he was himself. My local family connections made him hesitate to treat me as roughly as he treated village boys who dared trespass on railway property.

I answered him politely in my very best 'panloaf'. "Sir, I just wanted to make sure that Donald and Andy were OK. It was a near miss. Old Meggie was lucky".

Angus stared at me with an odd expression and gripped me by the shoulder. He smelled of whisky.

"Lucky yuh say! Mah God! A near miss? What div ye think that is?" and extended his index finger. I looked at Donald and Andy together on their footplate and concluded that Angus must have been 'celebrating' very early that morning. The stationmaster relaxed his hold and gave me a shove in the direction of the station offices.

"At least yuh kin mak' yersel' usefu' so rin back an' ask P.C. Rae tae phone Inverbarrow for an ambulance. And we'll be needin' Doctor McFadden. It looks tae me as if we've some casualties. Dinna jis' stan' there, boy! Hurry up!"

Inverbarrow, the next sizeable town up the line, had a hospital. Ignoring Angus's rough tone, I waved Donald and Andy farewell, but they were busy watering Meggie with the stout leathern hosepipe hanging down from its bracket, so I went into action immediately and galloped back till I ran into the station staff, including Reuben the senior porter, Tam Wilson his helper, Moira the ticket-clerk and Cushnie the guard, all standing around with ashen faces. I told them that all was well but that Mr Macdonald wanted an ambulance for the casualties and to send for Doctor McFadden, who was the local GP.

Cushnie, who had been waiting with his flags for *Meldrum Meggie* to back up to the main line platform and couple on to his two carriages for the 9.21 to Monymuir, asked me snappishly, "Casualties? Fitta like casualties is that? Fa's been hurtit up yonder? Did ye nae see Donald an' Andy?"

Yes, I'd seen them both. They were OK, Meggie too, I kept telling the anxious group what I believed to be fact. Grandad insisted I return to the house and look after my Granny. I found her knitting in her rocking-chair and started to tell her about the engine and how Donald and Andy had polished the metalwork until it shone like the rising sun but she seemed to know what had really happened and murmured, softly, "Aye, they cleaned Meg for her last journey".

I thought she was "wandering", an expression Grandpa sometimes used when her habitual vagueness irritated him. He appeared an hour later, grim-faced and addressed me without his pronounced Scots accent, something he only did when he was angry.

"What do you mean telling everybody that everything was OK? OK you say? Dammit, your engine pals were killed! Done for. Kaputt. The one solitary consolation is that that damn Jerry crashed near Banff."

My grandmother, over seventy, who claimed Highland ancestry and with it second sight, tried to defend me but was soon crushed. The nor'east women of that late Victorian generation didn't argue with their husbands.

The next week proved a remorseful period. I believed that the whole world was laughing at me and stayed off school again, using my earlier illness as an excuse. I just wanted to go back to London. Angus Macdonald made it clear that I was a stupid little mischief-maker deserving of a good thrashing. He himself had found the bodies of poor Donald and Andy standing upright in what remained of the roofless engine-cab. McFadden the doctor had said they had died immediately from the effects of "blast" and couldn't have felt any pain.

Hearing this, Angus told everybody that in his opinion the two men could not possibly have survived for a moment, so that my story of seeing them alive and talking to them must be fantasy or more likely just an attempt to attract attention.

"Wha should ken better? Himsel' or a loon o' twalve?" He, Angus, had been first on the spot and had seen the extent of the damage right away. That auld engine had been wrecked and certainly couldn't have moved. So he said and everyone believed him.

I had read about bomb blast, a sort of shock-wave produced by the rapid movement of air after the bomb explosion, a phenomenon known to produce peculiar results. Death without visible injury was one of them. I could offer no explanation for what I'd seen but I knew I'd seen it.

Few agreed with Angus Macdonald that I was to be blamed for carrying what he called scathingly "a wicked false report". After all, I had passed on the word about fetching the ambulance and the doctor. The station staff had known me from summer holiday visits and were without exception kindly disposed, especially Moira the sixteen-year-old ticket-clerk in her first job. "Hadn't the wee English laddie been poorly? Didn't he used to play around that engine wi' Donald and Andy? Must hae been a terrible shock tae him. He just couldna face up to seein' them deid!"

One person only believed my story and that was Granny. She said that "they were sayin' goodbye". A child was sometimes privileged to bid farewell to departing spirits just as they were about "to pass over". Grandad told her roughly not to fill the boy's head with such rubbish but grudgingly admitted that based on his own memories of the trenches perhaps I just might have seen their corpses erect in the cab stiffened in death though the rest was the product of "a kid's imagination" and he didn't want to hear another word on the subject. Grandma never referred to it again.

When I got better Moira the ticket-clerk told me "in confidence" that Angus MacDonald had been "on the carpet" at Head Office because he had been absent from his duties when the bomb dropped. Actually, she explained, looking over her shoulder, he'd been drunk. Nobody was sorry when he was "transferred", a polite term for demotion.

Donald and Andy were buried in the Auld Kirkyaird at Monymuir. A nameless D-40 worked the branch line but I never got to know the crew. Father came back from Dunkirk and was given a Staff posting to Edinburgh. He enrolled me in a select boarding-school in that fair city and from there I entered the Medical School.

Although many years have elapsed since I saw my boyhood friends looking down at me from Meggie's footplate, I can still picture them in my mind's eye, readying their glittering charge for her last journey. Theirs were the only ghosts I ever met, not spectral beings, but rather stolid, just as in life. I like to think that it was for my benefit alone that Meggie had appeared proud and strong, on the very threshold of her disintegration.

But Meggie wasn't taken away from human ken forever, not completely. After the war, when the Kinlonie branch line had been demolished in the name of Beeching, a reborn Meggie, expertly restored, went on permanent display at the Locomotive Museum at Inverbarrow. Whenever I come up from London I drop in at the Museum to pay my respects to my old friend.

I visited the two graves at Monymuir only once. They were overgrown and sadly neglected. On that singular occasion I was coming out of the lych gate when an old man passed me and muttered "Doctor Watson I presume". The fact that my name is Watson and that I am a long-standing member of the healing profession didn't help to lessen the shock.

9. *Brotherly Love*

The hall was ill-lit. Excellent. Ghosts flourish best in semi-darkness. At my annual lecture the audience was small but, as always, select and (I hoped) had a genuine interest in the subject. I dispensed with a formal welcome and, when the rustling and the coughing ceased, acknowledged their polite applause.

My plan was to start with a short preamble on the essential qualities of ghost stories and then tell them one of my own, demonstrating an original narrative technique. I had always found this to work. This year I'd chosen *Brotherly Love* as my title. This was intentionally ironic, since fraternal affection is hard to detect in this tale of family life recalled from the early years of the century. In a ghostly narrative it's an accepted convention to blur the timescale and set the action well back in the past.

"For my hearers' benefit I should explain that classic ghost stories may be arranged into half-a-dozen identifiable types. The antiquary Montague Rhodes James wrote over thirty in what has come to be a much-imitated style. The best of his phantoms were never ethereal, wispy forms but solid bony manifestations of physical horror which lie in wait patiently for centuries until a chance action or discovery unleashes their potential for harming the living. One of the most frightening made itself out of bed-clothes which gradually take threatening form after a Cambridge Professor finds a bronze whistle on a Norfolk shore and blows it.

I read a passage from Dr James's story 'Oh, Whistle and I'll Come to You, My Lad'. When I'd finished somebody in the hall blew a low note on a whistle. No-one laughed or took any notice.

"Incidentally," I continued, "bedclothes play a significant part in my story, which concerns a distinguished family of four brothers named duBellay. Their mother had died in childbirth. The surviving child was now three and in poor health. Father was an Army Colonel attached to War Office Intelligence When they weren't away at school the boys were left in the charge of a Mr and Mrs Fred Lear. Lear styled himself butler but was really little more than an odd-job man. Mrs Lear, a hard-faced young woman more than twenty years her husband's junior, ran the affairs of the house, which stood in spacious grounds within easy reach of London in, shall we say, Hampshire. It's not a good idea to pinpoint actual places but I refuse to call it Blankshire, like some writers. Not that it matters after all this time, but I'll prefer to disguise their address and call it Hallow House, Gillis Hill, a seventeenth-century manor on the outskirts of a market town."

Someone laughed. Rather a nasty laugh, I thought. Who on earth could find anything amusing in that?

"Of course, you'll understand that the writer of an uncanny tale has to place it against the right background. Setting is always of paramount importance. Buildings erected on Saxon foundations and granges encroaching on a graveyard are ideal, as are crumbling castles, deserted beaches and narrow paths through woods. It's a challenge to find a novel venue these days. Hallow House, an ancient pile set in a ten-acre estate with a family vault where past duBellays rested, might have been built for the benefit of ghosts. You could easily lose your way in its labyrinth of panelled rooms or expect to meet something shrouded shuffling along the corridors…"

Another laugh, more of a cackle. I shall disregard it.

"You'll know that Gillis was originally Gil's, an old name for the Devil that indicates a former place of ill-repute. A well-used gibbet, witches' sabbaths and walking dead 'uns, all that sort of thing. The folk memory in those parts is strong, even now. Anyone over the age of sixty could tell you a ghost or haunted house story about Gillis Hill."

That whistle again and a moaning sound. I peered into the gloom but couldn't spot the source of the nuisance which seemed to have come from the darkest corner of the hall.

"Hallow House had been the family seat of the duBellays since time immemorial. They claimed Anglo-Norman descent. For some reason their father had bestowed classical names on the children. The youngest was christened Lucian and his brothers, in ascending order of seniority, were Julian, Dorian and Adrian. After their mother died the Colonel advertised for domestic staff to replace the old devoted couple who had left within a week of her death. The Lears took over the running of Hallow House and attended to the immediate needs of the older boys when they were home from school. Mrs Adeline Lear was more than just an efficient housekeeper. The Colonel had an eye for the ladies and she soon proved herself, shall I say, a valuable asset during his weekend visits from the War Office.

"A bout of rheumatic fever had left Lucian with a serious heart weakness. He was a shy, nervous child, in the constant care of the local doctor, an old Scot named Fergus McIntosh. The two elder brothers were inclined to play tricks on him, nothing particularly hurtful, but considering his frail condition they ought to have been more considerate. In earlier years Julian had also suffered at their hands but in course of time had learned to stand up for himself. Mrs Lear took little heed of these minor escapades. "Boys will be boys; a time-honoured excuse for mischief," as she said.

"Boys will be boys will be boys will be…" A jeering high-pitched voice echoed the sentence. "Not much of a joke was it, that old game?"

This was contemptible. Shrugging my shoulders I remarked that so-called practical jokes were sometimes adopted by writers as a fictional background for tales of supernatural visitants intruding into our world, often using children as intermediaries. I paraphrased a distinguished novelette by Henry James, an American and no relation to our own English Montague of like surname. Then I snapped back at my persecutor. Attack is said to be the best defence.

"Funny you should mention that, sir, since I was just about to embark on the main part of my story, which does indeed bring in an old game. So if you wouldn't mind waiting until I've finished I should be delighted to receive your comments."

Toujours la politesse. It worked. Silence from the floor. Good. I fielded that one nicely. Somewhere outside the hall I could hear a child crying, or it may have been a cat. I took up the narrative again.

"Back we go fifty years to the winter of 1914. Chills, a full moon, wreaths of snow on the ground and a night without a breath of wind. Dorian was telling the others an appropriate bedtime story about the Highland soldier killed on the battlefield whose animated corpse returns from the grave to get revenge on a wicked cousin who had cheated him out of the family fortune. In a hoarse whisper Dorian painted an uneasily graphic picture of the rotting skeleton, dropping earth from its tattered kilt, lurching into the swindler's chamber at midnight with his bonneted skull peering over the bedrail showing hollow eye-sockets. He may have got the gruesome picture from a nightmarish short story, 'Thurnley Abbey', though the returner theme is as old as the Greeks.

"Hollow, hollow, hollow eye-sockets, hollow house ... Hallow house ... don't you remember Hallow House!" echoed through the hall.

Dammit, I hadn't quelled the nuisance after all. Apart from a low muttering, no-one in my audience had so far protested and I now had good reason to believe that this was no ordinary heckler.

"Mrs Lear's handbell summoned the three elder duBellays to supper in the kitchen at the precise moment when Dorian's tale was poised to reach its grisly climax. The child Lucian was predictably frightened and started to cry. Her dull husband led the tearful child out, leaving the tale unfinished. Dorian, who disliked having his performances upstaged, started to protest but Mrs Lear's threat of an adverse report to the Colonel reduced the youth to pained silence during the meagre meal.

"The interrupted *dénouement* of his story encouraged Dorian to develop a plan of action which would complete its telling. This involved a hoax known to many past generations of children, though one might think that Adrian at seventeen was old enough to know better than to take part in such a charade. When the house was quiet, all three brothers would dress up in bedsheets borrowed from the linen-cupboard and play "ghost" in Lucian's bedroom. Julian tried to back out but was told not to be a poor sport. Adrian suggested that the sinister effect would be enhanced if the shrouded figures danced round Lucian's bed in a ring which, he informed them, was a fashion of the undead.

"Undead! Undead! How does it feel to be undead?"

Now I really was angry. I resolved to flush out the heckler once and for all. Another direct assault was called for; not so polite this time.

"Sir, I do not know. Perhaps you'd care to come up and relate a story of your own rather than plague us with your constant rude interruptions!"

No response again, but my audience resumed their muttering, louder this time. I squinted into the gloom of the hall again, looking for my interlocutor and decided that the culprit might well be a small, muffled-up personage slumped apart from the rest in the back row.

A well-dressed man sporting a spotted bow tie raised his hand. Oh dear, not another one. This wasn't going well. But this gentleman was excessively polite.

"Excuse me sir, but to whom were you speaking? I assure you that nobody here has interrupted your talk".

His comment brought out a chorus of agreement.

I'll pass over the next couple of minutes of acute embarrassment while I apologised and did my best to recover the storyline. This appeared to amuse everybody and the muttering began again. I noticed that the little muffled-up chap seemed to have moved forward into another row nearer the front. I realised that details from my story which I hadn't yet revealed to the audience were merging with those from the old tale by Dr James. A fat man in a dark-blue uniform asked if I was "feeling all right". I ignored him and carried on.

"As was their habit, the Lears retired at ten o'clock, turning the gaslight low. When Adrian was sure that the coast was clear he led the other two down to the linen-cupboard in the basement where they nervously girded themselves for action. Wrapped in cotton bedsheets and with towels wound around their heads this trio of mock-phantoms climbed the stairs and passed silently along the dark corridors until they reached the door of Lucian's small bedroom. Julian's heart was beating fast. He was finding no joy in this game.

"Adrian edged the door open. They could hear the child's regular breathing and trod cautiously. Their victim was not to be startled out of his slumbers just yet. Dorian was trying not to giggle but Julian had a premonition of disaster. Dorian's gothic-horror tale of the skeleton with its empty eye-sockets peering over the end of the bed flashed into his mind and he breathed a silent prayer to his personal god, the deity of escaping the consequences...

"But it was too late to turn the clock back. They were already inside Lucian's room. The child's nightlight flung their distorted shadows against the plaster wall. The outline of his narrow couch was barely visible but the near-darkness was relieved by a pale shaft of moonlight shining through a narrow gap in the curtains, allowing the shrouded intruders to see that their little brother was fast asleep.

"On Adrian's signal they joined hands and began to move, noiseless in their stockinged feet. It was certainly effective, a good trick. Try to imagine the sight? – three spectral white-draped figures dancing rhythmically around the bed, with three corresponding shadows moving in slow motion across the wall. The trailing sheets swished and shone in the rays of the new moon.

I could see that my audience had been caught up in the macabre thrill, so to relieve their tension I inserted a footnote for the audience and informed them of the obvious fact that shadows and moonbeams were frequent props in the best ghost stories. My example was Mrs Molesworth's 'The Shadow in the Moonlight', set in a big country manor not unlike Hallow House. She was a late Victorian writer of childrens' stories who occasionally launched out into the uncanny with great effect. One or two of the heads nodded wisely and I took up the tale again. A rhyming couplet remembered from prep school drifted into my brain.

"Trip it, trip it, as you go / On the light fantastic toe
Light fantastic ... Quack, quack!"

This is truly awful. Now I'm making a noise like a duck. Their laughter was deafening and cruel too. They must think I'm losing my sanity but I mustn't give in. I clapped my hands and the duck flew away. That child outside was crying again though now the mournful sound seemed to be coming from a distance. I willed myself to continue.

"Dorian could not contain himself any longer and deliberately uttered a sepulchral moan. The little boy stirred. Can any of you imagine what alien images must have burst into his childish mind when his eyes blinked open? *Une belle horreur!* Close by his bed arose shifting phantoms from the depths of his worst nightmare. Here was Dorian's tale of nocturnal terror come true, ghastly sheeted things from the grave, gliding silently round and round, shapeless heads bobbing, hands joined in a ring. He tried to hide under the quilt but his scrabbling fingers would not obey him. The circling apparitions moved closer until the tallest of them reached out and actually touched his face with a clammy finger. He tried to scream for help but from whom? From his brothers? Not possible. He was trapped by supernatural beings. A violent paroxysm of coughing racked his small body and then…"

At that crucial point my highly-coloured and carefully-worded narrative was interrupted by an awful screech, like a banshee from hell. I covered my ears until its reverberations had died away and resumed in a trembling voice…

"The 'ghost' who had broken the fatal circle was Adrian. The protective ring had now become a short procession of three with Julian bringing up the rear. It was then that Julian became conscious of *four* dancing shadows, one with clawing hands outstretched, flickering on the bedroom wall. He noticed with a shudder that this last shape was definitely blacker than the other three and like nothing he had seen before. What new visitor had come into the bedroom? Julian dared not look behind him to see what it might be. A frightful fiend, perhaps? He had read *The Rime of the Ancient Mariner.*

"You've broken the ring," he croaked. "There's something else here, behind me! An extra shadow. It came off the wall".

"Broken the ring? Something else behind you? Extra shadow?" came Adrian's irritated voice from the gloom. It lacked his usual confidence.

"I think … I saw it." This from Dorian. "A kind of long flapping shape gliding down from the wall. The nightlight's gone out. Someone light the gas. I don't like this silly game. Come on Adrian, please let's chuck it."

Adrian was glad of an opportunity to draw back and save face. "All right. I've got matches," he answered. Fumbling with a box of Vestas he managed to light one of the gas jets by the mantel-shelf. It gave out a popping noise and flooded the room with a pure white radiance.

In the moment it took for his vision to adjust to the sudden flare of gaslight Julian caught the fleeting image of what looked like a tall white pole with a small round head and black button eyes leaning against the bedroom door. At first he thought it must be Adrian or Dorian in a sheet but then he saw the two of them looking frightened and realised that whatever it was by the door was not part of their game. His hair stood on end, something which we are told happens in moments of extreme terror but the others didn't appear to notice the apparition, which slowly melted away.

"Adrian peered at the child and turned to Dorian. 'Lucian's very quiet. Look, his lips are, sort of, blue' he said. 'Looks as if the poor little swine is sick again. Dorian, you'd better get the Lears down.'

'I'm going,' muttered Dorian. In the bright light his face was ashen. Looking around uneasily and trailing his sheet he made for the door and ran straight into Mr Lear, clad in a nightshirt and carrying a lantern.

'Master duBellay! You should be in bed! Is there something wrong? I'll call Adeline.' But at that moment his wife appeared in the doorway in hair-curlers and a dressing-gown.

'What are you boys doing in here? What silly prank is this?' Her mouth opened when she saw the still head on the pillow. Only Julian broke the silence. He was practically hysterical.

'I saw it! I saw it!' he kept repeating, 'a tall white thing with little eyes. It looked at me.'

Mrs Lear had been examining the child. Her eye lighted on the brothers' "ghost" attire.

'So there's your ghost is it?' She clapped her hands. 'Be quiet, all of you! He's not breathing. Look… there's blood round his chin.'

There was a hushed pause while she held a hand-mirror to the child's open mouth. The glass remained clear.

'I think he's dead,' she whispered. 'We'd better get the doctor.'

Mrs Lear was undoubtedly considering her own future. Adrian gave her an edited account of their masquerade.

'Just a joke,' he insisted, with a sheepish grin.

She soon came to a decision. 'This'll have to be reported right away, but first we'll get rid of these…" She gathered up the bedclothes and told the shrinking trio that so far as she could see their stupid game had frightened their little brother so much that he'd suffered a fit. His weak heart could not stand it and he had died. It was an accident, but they could all land in the direst trouble unless they told the doctor the same story and stuck to it when they were questioned later.

"Tell me the same old story. Same old story".

Another uninvited comment. That uncomfortable thought crawled back into my mind. Was I just confusing the fictional images of my narrative with the reality of the present? The fellow had swivelled his head around in my direction but I didn't care to see his face so I averted my gaze and returned the audience to the bedroom scene in Hallow House.

"Thus it was agreed that not a single word should be uttered about their ghostly joke. Not a hint. After supper they had gone to bed. No-one had been in Master Lucian's room except Mrs Lear herself. She had made her usual round to make sure that Master Lucian was asleep and had found him in the throes of a fit. Her husband had tried to revive him but it was too late. He had gone for the doctor immediately. '...and you Julian, remember, above all nothing about black shadows or whatever you mistakenly thought you saw. You were each in your own bedrooms, never here. Now off you go!'

"In their agitated state, with their little brother's lifeless body limp, it was not surprising that the three duBellay brothers swiftly agreed with one voice to take her advice. Mrs Lear sent her husband to bicycle to the village and rouse their old family doctor, Fergus McIntosh. Complaining about the lateness of the hour, Dr Fergus eventually rattled up the long drive to Hallow House in his pony trap. Shaking his head sadly he listened to Mrs Lear's account of Lucian's last moments. 'The puir wee lad had suffered a heart-seizure. Painless. It was always on the cards', he told them.

"When the Colonel, summoned urgently from London, returned to Hallow House by train he was overcome but, supported by the sympathetic presence of Mrs Lear, did not question the essential truth of what he was told. His three sons sat silent. After a routine inquiry, Lucian's death was attributed to natural causes. Dr Fergus's professional judgment was not questioned and the child was interred in the family vault alongside his mother.

"As time passed the emotional impact of that terrible night gradually lessened but the shock of Lucian's sudden death, that "extra shadow" on the wall, the unseen presence behind him, and the "tall white pole" by the door were never far from Julian's mind. Adrian, older, less imaginative and made of sterner stuff, soon absolved himself from any responsibility for the tragedy. For him it had been brought about by force of circumstances when a harmless schoolboy prank had misfired. Dorian, younger and more romantic, wondered if Julian had caught a fleeting glimpse of the Angel of Death. Adrian, a stalwart non-believer in such entities, explained Julian's apparition as the branch of a tree waving in the wind and throwing its shadow against the bed-room wall. Nor would he accept that the shape by the door could be anything other than an optical effect set off by the sudden glare of bright gaslight. Plausible, but neither Julian nor Dorian were wholly convinced. The curtains, Julian recalled, had been almost completely drawn leaving space only for a thin shaft of moonlight to enter. After that one discussion caution prevailed. It would not do to let the Colonel or even the Lears hear such talk.

Adrian persuaded himself and Dorian that their version of events represented, if not quite the absolute truth, something close to it. But for Julian the images of that winter were reassembled in nightmares and for weeks afterwards he fled through endless dream corridors pursued by a pack of cloaked horrors with button eyes. In time he might have confessed his guilt feelings to his father but Adrian's restraining counsel overwhelmed his scruples. Besides, important events were looming in Europe and Colonel duBellay was now rarely at Hallow House. Mrs Lear's position was greatly strengthened and in the Colonel's increasingly protracted absences she ruled Hallow House with a heavy hand.

"In August of that year the Great War broke out. The Colonel was too old to go to the front. He enjoyed life at the War Office until his luck ran out and he was killed in the very last air-raid on London, in May 1918. Adrian, who was in his School Training Corps, volunteered immediately, left for France in 1915 and fell at the Battle of the Somme, leading his platoon. By the terms of the Colonel's will, Dorian and Julian inherited Hallow House and what remained of the family fortune. The Lears continued as caretakers of Hallow House. Julian aspired to enter politics and went up to Oxford to read for the Bar. Dorian, keen to follow in his father's footsteps, entered Sandhurst and was marked out for a regiment in India.

"But tragedy was to strike the family yet again. Dorian duBellay, who was at home on terminal leave and both the Lears perished when Hallow House was partially destroyed by fire. Rumours were rife, but it was not established what caused the conflagration and in the end the local police put it down to a gas explosion, probably caused by Fred Lear's carelessness. Julian, plagued by remorse because he had not been on the scene when disaster came, never returned to live in Hallow House, although he had it rebuilt and turned into a children's home, renamed Holly Lodge. What happened to him, you may ask? Where is he now?"

At last the time has come for me to reveal my secret.

"Perhaps you have already guessed it. I – note the first person – had started to canvass for the Liberal Party candidate in a North London borough election, but after my brother died in the fire at Hallow House I started hearing strange voices. When they started to interrupt my speeches I had to stand down and give up any hope of a public career. Fortunately my inheritance enabled me to live independently and write supernatural fiction. Note that I refer to "*my* brother" and "*my* speeches" because you must surely have realised after witnessing the painful distractions during my reading that I myself, the very man you see before you, am Julian, the last of the duBellays. I am grateful to the authorities for allowing me to address you. Thank you all for your patient attention. You have been a model audience."

'With one exception,' I might have added. After polite applause a long silence followed my abrupt conclusion. No-one spoke up about those interruptions. Evidently they had heard nothing. Of course they hadn't. That vengeful voice is meant for me alone. That muffled personage had definitely gone, for good I hoped. I was relieved. There was something menacing about him – or 'it' – gradually advancing from one row to the next.

I invited questions. A man in a dog-collar asked if these happenings at Hallow House had any basis in real life. Did the renamed manor still exist? Had there really been a fire and fatalities there? Did the voices start before or after the fire? Were there no living relatives of this aristocratic duBellay family? A mean-looking woman in a feathered hat picked up irregularities in the ages of the brothers and stupidly asked how old I was, saying that the real Julian must be at least sixty now. I couldn't possibly be him. That annoyed me. Fortunately, a burly fellow in a dark-blue uniform stepped in and got her to hold her peace. I assured doubters like her that since what they'd heard was fiction, questions of that sort were pointless and tried to shift discussion to a more elevated plane. She looked as if she might defy the blue uniform but a silver-haired old man, perhaps her husband, persuaded her not to start such an unpromising argument. He relieved the tension by asking me if Mrs Lear might have started the fire?

I didn't know. They were all just characters in an uncanny tale. Such tales tend to leave loose ends and small details unexplained.

Could the additional black shadow have been a daemonic manifestation of the character Julian's feeling of guilt, enquired a sad-looking fellow. The dog-collar disagreed. It was undoubtedly an evil spirit after Julian's soul, but fortunately unable to defeat the angel, manifested in the form of a white pole. He quoted a verse from the second chapter of the Book of Revelation, something about being cast into prison by the Devil but I didn't see what that had to do with anything in my story.

Angels and demons? The path their debate was taking was far too theological for me. I reminded the audience once again that what they'd heard was simply an invention – an ingenious fiction created for their entertainment – and that they were entitled to put on it whatever construction they pleased. This year they were showing themselves even more slow-witted than usual.

I must have sounded testy as the burly man in the blue uniform told the audience that it was time for the meeting to end. Two younger blue uniforms appeared and escorted me from the hall. I glanced back over my shoulder and a chill of fear enveloped me – for there was that sinister white pole, propped up against the backdrop of the stage, with little button eyes staring down at the audience. It must have been right behind me all the time I was speaking. And that wasn't all. Lolling by the exit was the muffled-up presence. I don't think it was a normal person. I'm no coward but as I passed I kept my eyes shut. I told the man in charge not to let either of them attend my lecture ever again and he agreed.

~ ~ ~

When the story-teller had been taken out a bald-headed man in a superior dark-blue uniform and wearing an impressive row of medal ribbons climbed on to the platform and introduced himself as Major Burgess. He explained that their speaker was an interesting case driven to bury his guilt under layers of fantasy. What he said was illuminating.

"His name isn't duBellay, of course. It's Eric Bowley, an only child. His real father was an Army private, wounded and captured at Dunkirk, spent the rest of the war in a German prison-camp. To make ends meet Mother Bowley did shift-work in a factory but later branched out into other activities in what you might call the Piccadilly entertainment business.

"Eric was evacuated from South London in 1939 and billeted with a couple of West Country chicken farmers by the name of Mr and Mrs Fred Lear. Not very charitable folk from all accounts. The Lears kept the boy away from school, used him as a hired help and didn't spare the rod. They had two sons, who gave him a hard time. After a while Eric took his revenge. He set fire to the farmhouse and ran off back to London. He was put in an institution.

"Dad came back from the prisoner-of-war camp, a husk of a man, in 1945. It was anything but a happy homecoming. The Bowleys lived in a dilapidated tenement off the Waterloo Road, about as far removed from Eric's grand Hallow House as this asylum is from Buckingham Palace. Eric burned down the tenement with his parents inside. He'd first battered them to death with a rather odd choice of blunt instrument, a chopped-off section of a tent-pole. Unfortunately there was a baby in the flat above and it died of asphyxiation.

Eric had a conscience. When he found that out he gave himself up. Under eighteen, so they couldn't hang him. Sent him here instead. Guilty but insane, to be detained at His Majesty's pleasure. That was fifteen years ago. Our doctors won't agree to his release and anyway how would a chap like him live outside? Write ghost stories? He only knows one and spends all his time perfecting it.

"By the way, duBellay was the family name of an old French nobleman who made up love sonnets. Eric's a great reader, self-educated of course. Helps in our library. Certainly has a talent, knows what goes to make a creepy tale believable. We let him unfold his latest version to invited guests on Open Days. He doesn't vary it much from one year to the next – his notion of an aristocratic family circle, playing ghost with his imaginary brothers, the apparitions in the bedroom , the remote colonel father-figure, a hint of resentment at Mrs Lear's status and those noisy interruptions which no-one hears but himself, not forgetting the crying child. It wasn't hard for the doctors here to understand where it all came from. We've heard of his muffled- up figure before but it's the first time he's ever mentioned the tall white pole looking down at us. That part at least is true. I saw it myself."

10. *A Window-Cleaner's Ghost Story*

Some may doubt the existence of a supernatural presence in this story, which relates to my short post-war career as a temporary assistant at an ancient Scottish University. I was formed by an even more ancient English one, where undergraduates appeared to take the strains of academic life lightly, even in the run-up to Finals. In Scotland they did not try so hard to conceal pre-exam tensions. This was particularly evident in the late 1940s, when ninety percent of students were mature ex-servicemen interrupted by the war, living on government grants and years behind in their studies. For most of them to get a good professional degree was all-important; a First or High Second was essential, and to drop to a Third was the ultimate disgrace.

One falling star of whom much might have been expected was Jamie Laurie. He had entered the Faculty of Arts straight from the local High School, where he had been a fair pupil. Jamie had but one distinction; he was the only begotten son of Sir David Laurie, chairman of a big corporation with world-wide interests in container shipping. The elder Laurie, himself a graduate of the University, knew that his offspring could never hope to emulate his own successful career and made no secret of Jamie's shortcomings. After his mother's death the boy's confidence evaporated. At the age of eighteen he was pronounced medically unfit for national service and suffered from a weakness of the spine which left him with a pronounced stoop. He was allowed to continue his studies as one of a minority of school-leavers and entered Ossian College to read for English Honours. For a couple of years he managed to hold his own but after a mediocre performance in the Intermediate Examination he was advised to revert to an Ordinary Degree course.

Jamie stubbornly chose to ignore this counsel, soon found himself out of his depth and started to rely on strong ale to keep the world at bay. Laurie senior, who spent most of his time commuting between London and Sydney, took little interest in his son's deteriorating performance. The young man, long-standing feelings of inferiority now well established, entered upon his last term knowing that his probable fate at the hands of the examiners was at best a Third.

I myself was never directly involved with Jamie, though he had occasionally appeared whey-faced at my unoriginal discourses on Modern Drama. He was one of those downtrodden characters who invited sympathy. Tom Allison, his supervisor, an ex-bomber pilot with a DFC to his credit, had given him additional coaching not so much out of the kindness of his heart than as a favour to Jamie's father whom he had known in the war and from whom he hoped to get strong support for a senior post in Australia.

Tom told me that his errant pupil hadn't turned in an essay for weeks. In those days there was no "continuous assessment" record and the class of degree depended entirely on the quality of the student's Finals papers, taken two *per diem* for five days, Monday to Friday. Such a gruelling regime wouldn't be tolerated nowadays but Finals discipline was then much more unforgiving, physically as well as mentally. In theory Jamie could still get his "First" with an unexpected show of genius, past sins forgotten. In reality, he didn't have a hope.

On the opening day of Finals I had been appointed invigilator, charged along with Tom Allison and several other members of the Faculty to maintain law and order. I noticed Jamie because he rushed in late and out of breath, trailing his conspicuous scarlet undergraduate gown. He stood out from the other candidates because on the rare occasions when he turned up at my lectures he proudly sported that same ink-stained garment, a mediaeval relic traditionally peculiar to Scottish universities but after the war practically discarded. He told everybody that it had belonged to his father.

The examination paper, demanding translations "into good modern English" from Anglo-Saxon and Old Norse, was waiting on the trestle tables and our twenty-one candidates were looking at the daunting sheet with gloomy faces. This early period, centred on the Germanic epic, was generally regarded as a bug-bear, feared by all and requiring more preparation than contemporary literature because the translation exercises were hard to fudge.

Recalling my own recent struggles, I knew exactly how the rows of former members of H.M. Forces felt as they sat trembling in the sixteenth century examination-hall, renamed the Lochgelly Hall by the Victorians and known familiarly as 'Golgotha'. Faculty statutes from time immemorial stated that no student under inquisition was permitted to depart this place of skulls until thirty minutes had elapsed. Jamie sat out his period of grace without putting pen to paper and crept out as the bell on the Croon Tower tolled the half-hour.

'That won't do you any good,' I thought. Our External Examiner was an unrelenting Saxonist who would demand a decent showing in his favourite subject. Jamie would have to do exceptionally well in the literature papers to make up for his neglect of *Beowulf*. But Jamie stayed only a little longer for the afternoon paper on 'Early Literature Excluding Chaucer'. I never understood why Chaucer should be thus excluded, but it so happened that Fergus McAdam, our ill-beloved Kilgour Professor of English Language and Literature, was a Chaucer Man who insisted on a separate paper on the poet to reflect his own scholarly interests. It was becoming clear that at this rate Jamie would be unlikely to get any kind of a degree and should be advised to withdraw, collect a medical certificate and retry his finals the following year. I made up my mind to get Tom Allison, with whom I was on drinking terms, to speak to Professor McAdam as soon as possible. McAdam was never an easy man to catch but I knew he would be on hand on the morrow for his beloved Chaucer.

In those days there was no such thing as organized counselling". Before the war, students had been allotted so-called "moral tutors" but the early intakes of ex-servicemen didn't think they needed moral tutoring and the practice had been allowed to drop. Thus when Jamie turned up twenty minutes late for Tuesday's Chaucer examination looking as though he hadn't slept, scrutinized the printed paper and immediately screamed out "O God! I canna' do it, I canna' do it!" the attitude of the other candidates was not particularly sympathetic. Jamie fled from the hall in a panic, muttering wildly and collided with no less a personage than Professor McAdam himself coming in to make sure that everything was going according to plan.

Jamie didn't stop to talk but continued his flight. Tom Allison went after him but soon returned giving the thumbs-down signal. Apart from Tom, none of the invigilators considered that the young man's aberrant conduct fell within their area of official responsibility once he had quitted the examination scene. As for the other twenty candidates for Honours, many of those who had just begun to tackle the first question appeared stolidly amused. Pleasure in the downfall of others is well recognised to be a prime source of human satisfaction. The Germans call it *Schadenfreude* but we have no single word in our vocabulary for this comfortable assertion of moral superiority. At any rate there was no doubt that Jamie's spectacular collapse elevated the spirits of the rest. This insouciance applied equally to Professor McAdam. When Tom came back empty-handed our Professor said that "the laddie had dreed his weird" and "wad just come tae regret his lack o' application".

Jamie failed to appear to deal with Spenser and the Tudors at the afternoon session, nor was he available to confront Milton And The Seventeenth Century on the Wednesday morning so Tom Allison telephoned his Hall of Residence at nine-thirty to be told that "Mr Laurie wasnae in his quarters". Tom immediately called the Principal and advised him that Sir David Laurie's son had abandoned Finals and couldn't be found.

However, Tom's conclusion was premature. When I arrived at the Lochgelly Hall to help distribute the numbered examination books for Paper Six on Shakespeare, to my surprise Jamie was already there, hunched in his designated place, body completely wrapped in his gown, pinched features half-concealed by the lined hood. His hands and wrists were blue with cold, although the sun was shining outside. I had never seen the poor fellow in such a state, clearly incapable of tackling the examination. I suppose I ought to have reported him but I didn't. Notwithstanding his condition Jamie was entitled to try his luck at the great Honours lottery. I laid the printed paper face down on the table and told him to "cheer up" but he did not answer.

Later I remembered one odd thing. None of his neighbours paid the slightest attention to this rather conspicuous individual as they took their places; a classic case of unenlightened self-interest by people too intent on their own fates to spare a thought for anyone else. I was glad that I'd kept my own counsel because a few minutes later I noticed that his place was vacant except for the printed examination paper and a virgin answer book.

The student at the nearest table, Jessica Denshing – a buxom maiden reputedly popular with the older ex-servicemen – was holding her nose and complaining about a nasty smell but I couldn't detect anything. Apparently she hadn't noticed his brief presence at the neighbouring table and nor apparently had anyone else.

Invigilators usually worked in shifts of an hour and a half. On that sunny afternoon it was my turn to take the first break, so I gave up worrying about Jamie and spent the time with T.S. Eliot on a bench in the scholars' garden. Just before three-thirty I noticed a student in a reddish gown about fifty yards away, hunched up by the wall of the Croon Tower. That round-shouldered posture identified him as our truant in flight from the Shakespeare paper.

What was an invigilator supposed to do in such circum-stances? Drag the slacker back? Talk to him like a Dutch Uncle? Report him to the Chief Invigilator? I called out "Mr Laurie!" and quickened my pace towards the Tower. I'm sure he muttered something like "I've been back" or "I'm comin' back" before slipping round the corner into the quadrangle. When I got there my quarry was not in sight.

However, on return to Lochgelly Hall I found a completed script on Jamie's table. I took back my harsh words. Not only had he come back once more into the breach, so to speak, but he had finished the statutory three answers in an hour-and-a-half and a quick scan told me that his effort was more than compe-tent. This was a welcome surprise but he still had four more papers to face and at this rate of fall-out and absenteeism Jamie was sailing very close to the wind.

I replaced the script as I had found it for the Chief Invigilator to collect at the end of the session. Unfortunately this official happened to be the Rasmus Rask Reader in English Language and also Chief Internal Examiner, Dr Roland Dumbrill, a stickler for the rules, and on Sundays a lay preacher. This man didn't like me and the feeling was mutual.

I waited until the hall had cleared and casually mentioned Jamie to him – "I see our lost sheep has been and gone". Dumbrill looked blank. I explained that my reference was to Jamie Laurie who had walked out the day before. Dumbrill assured me pompously that the boy hadn't attended and had left no script. When I explained disingenuously that I'd actually seen him writing Paper Six and took Dumbrill over to Jamie's accustomed place, we found a numbered script and a faded scarlet undergraduate's gown on the seat. It was the worse for wear, muddy, torn in several places and soaking wet. I could have sworn that it hadn't been there when I came in. I turned it over and revealed a barely-decipherable name-tag, 'D. Laurie'.

Dumbrill looked suspicious and insisted that he had collected all the scripts directly from the candidates and couldn't have missed this one. I saw no reason to tell him that the writer had left early and had certainly not stayed anything like the full three hours. After an argument which just stopped short of a row he grudgingly added it to the pile, muttering "highly irregular" and flounced off, assuring me that I hadn't heard the last of this affair.

I appropriated the sodden gown and hung it on a peg in the students' cloakroom, intending to return it to Jamie if and when he chose to put in another appearance, but next day the peg was empty. Mrs Smith, the head 'skip' or cleaner assured me indignantly that she always kept the cloakroom locked at nights and that none of her domestics would dream of removing any garment.

On Thursday at nine o'clock I looked for Jamie in vain. The enemy that day, Pope and the Eighteenth Century, had always been regarded as the separator of sheep from goats. By nine-thirty he still had not materialised – a word which, with hindsight, I use advisedly. Nor did he return for the last three papers. Jamie had to be written off as a lost cause. After another call from Tom Allison, the Warden of Ossian College reported Jamie's absence to the police. The boy had achieved lost sheep status.

Sadly it didn't matter, anyway. On Saturday, following the last day of the examination, the *Evening Courant* announced that the partially-decomposed body of James Laurie, only son of the industrialist Sir David Laurie, had been found in the river by a man walking his dog. He had been dead for several days. Foul play was not suspected. Professor Fergus McAdam of the Kilgour Chair of English was shocked by the tragedy and had expressed profound sympathy to the family, stating disingenuously that his tutors had predicted that James would have been well in line for a First and a great future but had unfortunately suffered a breakdown during his Finals examination.

The verdict was one of accidental death by drowning. Suicide was never mentioned. McAdam gave one of his orotund performances at a Memorial Service in the College chapel, praising Jamie's brilliant performance as a student. He regretted this tragic end to a young life but, alas, thousands of young lives had been sacrificed in the War and survivors know full well how it feels to lose a comrade-in-arms. Most of Jamie's fellow-finalists attended. His father, who had flown in from Sydney for the inquest, shook hands with each of them at the door. The burial service a week later was private, though Tom Allison was included among the mourners. I was sure that after another month when the degree results were published Jamie would soon be no more than a fading memory.

This would certainly have been the case had it not been for the unexpected arrival at the Internal Examiners' meeting on the day after the funeral of Jamie's scripts for the last four papers, despatched from the Office of the Registrar and each plainly labelled with his correct candidate's number. Names were not used in Finals. Dumbrill was plainly embarrassed and assured McAdam that he had not seen them before and doubted their authenticity.

His discomfiture increased when Tom and the Shakespeare expert – a bony woman from Birmingham who maintained a permanent feud with Dumbrill – announced that were arguably "firsts", but Oscar Bruin, the External Examiner and an old salmon-fishing crony of McAdam's who turned up annually from Holland to create an impression of fair play and confirm the Internals' findings, was unwilling to grant Jamie more than a posthumous Third Class because he had not attempted the translations from Anglo-Saxon and Old Norse in Paper One.

McAdam looked dubious. Given the lad's record, the quality of scripts VII-X was obviously too high for Jamie to have reached. It looked to him as if somebody else had acted as proxy and submitted the last four on Jamie's behalf. "Possibly," he suggested with a malicious grin, "in return for some favour". At this Tom Allison banged the table and declared that his deceased pupil had produced a string of "alphas and beta plusses" in the previous two terms and that he himself would have predicted at least a high Second.

I was surprised to hear this optimistic attestation from Tom after what he had told me about Jamie's delinquency in the matter of tutorial essays, but all paled into insignificance when it emerged that the Shakespeare script which I had last seen in Dumbrill's possession was not available for review. The bony female from Birmingham accused Dumbrill of carelessness and hot words were exchanged.

My own lowly status in the Department did not allow me a place on the Internal Board but McAdam called me in to explain my altercation with Dumbrill. Dumbrill, as Chief Internal Examiner, was officially responsible for the security of all scripts and immediately started to whitewash himself by denying that Jamie had attended the examination so that the missing script couldn't have been written by him and that its loss was immaterial. McAdam agreed.

I described the ancient gown, with its "D. Laurie" label. This item of evidence ought to have matched my puny word against theirs and I held confidently to my original story in the face of attempts by McAdam and Dumbrill himself to get me to admit I was mistaken. I knew that Dumbrill was trying to cover up his own negligence and it was evident that McAdam, *ex-officio* Chairman of the Board, was not prepared to consider that the most insignificant member of his Department, namely myself, might be telling the truth about Jamie's presence. The pair closed ranks and dismissed the evidence of the tattered scarlet gown. According to Dumbrill it might have been left by any undergraduate. When I asked what had happened to it Dumbrill said that no-one had claimed it so he'd put it with the rubbish. I knew that was a lie; I had hung it up in the cloakroom myself.

Tom Allison did his best to support me by saying that in his opinion the calligraphy of the other four scripts was "similar to Jamie's", whereupon Dumbrill jumped up and renewed his attack, telling everybody present with a sneer that although the police pathologist's report had officially established Wednesday morning as the latest time of death "our most junior colleague" claimed to have observed this unfortunate lad writing in the afternoon of that same day. Dumbrill said he had questioned some of the candidates sitting in that section of the hall but no-one else had seen Jamie. "Are we then to assume that we're dealing with a ghost or [ha, ha] a ghost-writer perhaps?"

Tom reminded McAdam that there was no getting over the solid fact that we had in our hands those completed scripts for the last four papers. I repeated what I knew to be the truth; that ghost or not I had seen Jamie lining up for the Wednesday afternoon paper on Shakespeare and that I had quickly scanned his answers in Dr Dumbrill's presence. I didn't see why I should tell them about Jamie's early departure. Tom asked sweetly that in view of my statement was there any reason to suppose that Jamie's performance on that now missing paper might not be up to the standard of the others?

McAdam didn't like this at all and Dumbrill, fuming with rage, even had the nerve to ask me if this were some sort of conspiracy. Tom lost his temper and walked out, though later he apologised to McAdam. He had a low opinion of Dumbrill but needed a decent testimonial for that coveted job Down Under and McAdam could be vindictive, though it seemed to me that on this issue the Professor preferred to distance himself from Dumbrill. At that point he directed the attention of the Board to our other twenty candidates. It was a good year and five Firsts were recommended. Two of them were Tom's pupils. Jessica Denshing got the only Third.

The Jamie problem was solved when McAdam and Bruin put their heads together and held a separate meeting, the outcome of which was an *ex cathedra* announcement that since the Board of Examiners had received "a substantial proportion" of the ten papers the dead student should be "Recommended for Unclassi-fied Honours with Distinction". No such *jejune* proposal for a degree had ever been gazetted in the annals of the Faculty. McAdam should never have got away with such a piece of blatant chicanery, but in those unenlightened days a Regius Professor supported by an External Examiner could exercise near-divine powers.

That ought to have been the end of the business but it wasn't. The second Friday in July was always marked as the date of the Annual Summer Graduation, held in the New Auchentosh Hall, the old one having been bombed in 1941. I took my assigned place in the back row together with the rest of the academic small fry and watched as the procession of Ordinary Arts graduates mounted the platform one at a time to receive the magic tap on the head from the Principal. Classics and Philosophy were in the vanguard of the smaller Honours group, followed by modern European languages. English Language and Literature brought up the rear.

At the bottom of the official list my eye caught an entry in italics. Entries were italicised when there was something unusual about the person graduating, such as a previous degree from another university or when the recipient was unable to attend in person in which case *in absentia* was normally appended.

The list contained only one italicised item: *with Honours [unclassified with distinction] to James Laurie (decd.).* The absurd entry brought back the whole ghastly business. *In absentia* was omitted, an unusual oversight which struck me as curious in conjunction with the insertion of *decd.* Almost black humour.

Whether stimulated by association of ideas or by thinking of Jamie looking down from Heaven, or possibly looking up, I suffered a weird experience when my idle gaze focussed on the graduate at the tail end of the queue. Silhouetted against the sunlight beaming through a modern stained glass window his gown, like the others, appeared black but as the light faded I saw that it was really reddish. Graduates were expected to attend the ceremony in an ordinary black gown and the brighter colour made this wearer stand out from the procession of crows.

I detected something familiar about his stooping posture. Just then the ceremony was interrupted by a commotion in that same section of the auditorium. Our solitary Third, Jessica Denshing, seemed to be in the grip of hysterics. An attendant male nurse sought to calm her down as one of the marshals helped the terrified girl up the aisle to the exit.

In the meantime the Degree ritual had proceeded smoothly. The Dean had got to the end of our list and proposed Jessica's name "with Honours of the Third Class" in sepulchral tones but even as he spoke she had already been escorted out of the hall. Unhesitatingly and without expression he moved on to recite the final name on the register, that of "James Laurie, *in absentia*, with Honours unclassified with distinction". No spectre came out to ascend the platform and be greeted by the Principal. Jamie was dead and buried. The shape in the red gown, if it was ever there, had dissolved; a phantom created by the recollection of recent events, though not exactly in Wordsworthian tranquillity.

I found Tom Allison and the nurse commiserating with the panic-stricken girl in the midst of a crowd of the curious. She was not to be pacified. Waiting in the queue she had smelt something horrible and turned round to confront "Jamie, that boy who died, with a ghastly white face, covered up in that filthy old gown he used to wear".

Tom was sceptical at first and dismissed her uncanny tale as female hysteria and purely subjective, but what we later found on the floor by Jessie's chair made him, a man who'd survived two tours with Bomber Command, turn pale.

The wretched gown was now bone-dry. It has lost its colour and smelled strongly of earth. I put it in a paper bag and we repaired to the Funkhole, frequented by many generations of students, for a strong ale. There I told Tom the full story of whom or what I did see at the Shakespeare paper and whom or what I fancied I'd seen by the Croon Tower and at the Graduation Ceremony. He didn't laugh. Instead, he said we ought to destroy the stinking thing forthwith so we soaked it in petrol and made an end of the remnant. It took ages to burn.

When I produced my copy of the Graduation List and explained that the words *in absentia* had been omitted after Jamie's name, Tom pointed to the entry – and there it was, in plain Latin.

My own short contract as temporary Assistant Lecturer, by long tradition in the Kilgour Professor's gift, was not renewed. Dumbrill took a sabbatical. Sir David Laurie donated funds for a research scholarship in his son's name. Tom Allison went to a Chair in Australia. Although he kindly offered me a full lectureship in his new Department I decided that the perils of the academic profession were not for me and that I should try something less demanding and more profitable ... like window-cleaning.

11. *The Crocodile-Monster*

One Christmas The Writer of Fantastic Tales was entertaining his friend The Author of Classical Detective Stories.

"Has anyone ever told you that little gem of a story about the Institution Boy in the thirteenth bed, the one farthest from the door?" he enquired after the cigars and brandy had circulated.

Evidently nobody had, so The Writer continued with confidence.

"The setting," he began, "is a grim Institution more than a hundred years ago. After he calls "Lights Out" the candle is extinguished by the Dormitory-Master and the Institution Boy at the centre of our story – let us call him Peter – drifts off to sleep, shivering in his cold bed. He dreams that there is something coming in at the other end of the dormitory that shouldn't be. He tries to wake up but cannot.

"The room is too dark for him to make out the newcomer but he senses its alien character. It moves from the door to the first bed and stoops over the sleeping occupant. The dreamer understands that the occupant of the first bed may soon be "taken away" and the scene fades. At dawn he wakes up in a panic but to his relief everything in the dormitory looks normal and all the other boys, including the one in the bed nearest the oaken door, are sleeping peacefully.

"Peter in the bed furthest from the door is relieved to find it was only a delusion but on the next night the same sequence of events is repeated exactly as before, except that the intruder is now busying himself over the second bed. Peter still cannot see clearly what is going on but his awakening is less confident even though there is still no sign of any disturbance, but when the third and fourth beds are revealed in nightly succession as objects of this uncanny invader, the boy starts to fear its relentless advance from one bed to the next, every night closing the distance to his own.

"Moreover, his vision within the dream is becoming clearer. Out of the half-darkness the object of his fear is gradually assuming the shape of a creature vaguely reptilian with the scaly body of a crocodile. He knows it must have jaws and rows of terrible teeth. He names it the Crocodile-Monster.

"In daylight hours the frightened boy tells himself that this is just an absurd nightmare based on conventional images of the sort he can relate to witches' tales. At the same time he cannot deny that fear of his immediate future bordering on terror is beginning to control every waking hour. The prospect of what might happen to him when the Crocodile-Monster reaches the thirteenth bed fills his mind with dread.

"At first Peter is reluctant to reveal the nature of his fast-approaching predicament to the other boys and suffers increasing inner torment, further magnified by his childish imagination. On the fifth night he is afraid to fall asleep and stares at the solid oaken door until the Dormitory-Master puts out the candle. The dark shadows merge into the familiar dream and Peter shrinks back as another unsuspecting sleeper is attended to by the Crocodile-Monster.

"What the thing does after it reaches the bed of its apparent victim is not revealed to him as the dream always evaporates at that point but Peter is sure that the consequence for the other boys must be hideous beyond his powers of conception. Yet when he awakens all the beds are occupied and the bed-linen undisturbed as before.

"Peter decides that he must tell the others of this nightly visitant whose phantom depredations now seem to concern them all. No-one else has had such dreams but the boy in the sixth bed, frightened by Peter's excited warning that he is next to be taken by the Crocodile-Monster tells the Dormitory-Master, who issues a severe warning to Peter for spreading a childish and far-fetched story likely to upset the others. Any more such conduct, he promised, would merit a thrashing.

After this Peter becomes a convenient subject for ridicule levelled at him by the Dormitory-Master and a few of the inmates trying to curry that official's favour, but at dead of night his nocturnal visitant continues to appear through the door of his dream-dormitory and pursue its mysterious end.

The large room is no longer quite so dark and the menacing actions of the Crocodile-Monster are now more easily discernible in the crucial moment before the apparition gathers itself to attend to the remaining beds. When Peter awakens to find their occupants unharmed he becomes so confused as to compel the Dormitory-Master to summon the Nurse, who unsympathetically diagnoses a stomach-complaint and gives the ailing boy a dose of foul-tasting medicine.

Nevertheless Peter continues to alarm his fellows with the story of the fearful Crocodile-Monster, which provokes only their derision and finally annoyance. The exasperated Dormitory-Master gives him six painful strokes with the cane in front of the others. The jeers of his immediate neighbour in the twelfth bed increases Peter's distress. This boy, a feared bully, hits him in the face because he will not admit that the Crocodile-Monster is no more than a silly invention.

The Nurse reluctantly reports Peter to the Doctor, an easygoing slacker who prescribes a mild tranquillising potion and conveys him to the Institution Hospital for a couple of nights of observation in an otherwise empty ward. There Peter sleeps soundly but not dreamlessly. The Crocodile-Monster is able to penetrate the security of the ward but on this occasion does not advance far beyond the oaken door and soon melts into the gloom without approaching his bed. Peter fancies through the mist of his dream that perhaps its aspect may be less sinister than he had thought and wishes that he could have seen it more clearly. He does not think that it has teeth after all but continues to call it Crocodile-Monster for want of a more appropriate name.

On return to the dormitory Peter feels he has benefited from the change and almost begins to look forward to the nightly advent of the Crocodile-Monster, whose visitations to the hospital ward while in no way benevolent, now seem less weighted towards a personal threat. When the twelfth night arrives, much of the boy's apprehension returns and he tries to hold back from sleep as long as he can, but in the end he cannot resist the beguiling power of Morpheus to lure him away from his daytime problems, particularly since the Nurse had surreptitiously slipped another tranquillising dose into his glass of milk.

For the first time since he began to experience these dreams, Peter enjoys an almost completely uninterrupted slumber, totally free of the inhibiting presence of the Crocodile-Monster, but when he awakens, with a strangely renewed sense of well-being, he still retains a hazy recollection of a strange flapping sound, like the swish of bedsheets being flung off and the noise of a door closing.

On opening his eyes, he looks along the row of thirteen beds to find the one next to his own stripped and its occupant, the bully, gone. The others could not tell him what had befallen the bully but he was never afterwards subjected to their petty persecutions nor did he dream of the Crocodile-Monster that night, or any other night.

The Author of Classical Detective Stories waited patiently to hear more but his host had finished his narrative. Eventually the former broke the silence.

"I knew it! You fantasy-writers! No proper explanations! So that really *is* the end? Of course it is. What else should we readers expect? But I have questions! For instance, if the boy in the next bed is found horribly mutilated that would be a predictable horrific ending leaving us to ask who murdered him and for what reason. Why him and not Peter? Why does your Crocodile-Monster lose some of its threatening aspect? You tell me that Peter hears the strange sound only one night before he thinks the creature is due to descend on him? What is it? Could it be a final warning or a farewell? The closing of the door – does that signify that the Crocodile-Monster isn't coming back? So presumably Peter doesn't dream at all on the thirteenth night either, gets up as usual and never has that nightmare again.

"That would be a Happy Ending," commented the Writer of Fantastic Tales. "Unexpected, and not a bad finish."

"No, that would be a meaningless anti-climax," answered the Author of Classical Detective Stories, a stickler for logical explanations. The Author had little patience with fantastic tales: too many loose ends, he felt, and no pressure on the narrator to explain them away. This Crocodile-Monster was, he said, an absurdity. Crocodiles were not very attractive creatures but they're not really monsters of horror, just dangerous repulsive fast-moving reptiles. "Everybody knows what they look like and every child who's been to a zoo has seen one. Wouldn't a shapeless misty thing which gradually takes a definite ugly form, like a chimera, with wings and claws, be more in your usual phantasmagorical style? Does the tranquilliser get rid of Peter's nightmare? And surely the number thirteen has some obvious significance? Thirteen beds and you put Peter in the unlucky thirteenth, farthest from the door. How are you going to account for that unless you give it a happy ending?" he demanded triumphantly.

"That's not fair," answered his host with some asperity. "I didn't invent it. In fact I doubt if the basic plot ever had a named author. It's just a traditional creepy story grown through the years in a closed community, rather like those old supernatural ballads. Every generation adds a bit extra. Many of them were about malevolent ghosts. Didn't need a battery of explanations and neither does this."

After that exchange The Writer of Fantastic Tales bade farewell to his guest the Author who suggested that he might usefully apply his undoubted creative faculties to the finding of a more satisfactory conclusion.

In the past the Writer had hit on useful ideas for plots while dozing in bed so, after a generous nightcap, he retired and allowed his thoughts to wander among the details of the Dormitory story. Hearing the swish of bedsheets – what might have caused that? A closing door? Something breaking in on Peter's sluggishly returning consciousness? Bedsheets? What other kind of sheets might it have been?

Ah, it came to him. How about sheets worn by a corpse – a shroud? Eureka! He had it! This place was obviously a Dickensian Institution for unwanted male children. Suppose the boy in the next bed to Peter's had died and been removed silently so as not to alarm the others. How had he died? A heart-seizure? Neglect? Peter's dreams had always found the other beds undisturbed in the morning and their occupants awakening to another day. Only he, one Chosen Boy who escaped, had been permitted to know that his Crocodile-Monster was still seeking its prey, discarding one choice after another until it reached the twelfth bed, from which Peter's bullying neighbour, the sceptic who denied the existence of such a creature, was taken, that is, had his life taken.

Peter, and the reader, were left with only one fragment of evidence, the swish of sheets as the corpse was wrapped up and furtively carried out of the oaken door for immediate burial, with the slack Doctor issuing the death-certificate. After all, in those candle-lit days nobody looked too closely at what went on in an Institution of this type and the occasional fatality might well be treated as routine, a subject for quick disposal.

For Peter the thirteenth bed was a lucky one. That time he had been spared. Our Writer of Fantastic Tales now understood that the Crocodile-Monster could be quite simply explained as a small boy's image of Death and resolved to revise his bedtime story accordingly before he told it again.

12. *Elfride Awaits*

In the summer of 1938 a well-connected American gentleman of independent means, whom we shall call Charles Bentley, on vacation in the popular South Coast resort of Briscombe, came out of the rain to visit a young artists' exhibition organized by the Women's Institute in aid of local charities. It was mounted in a marquee within the grounds of St Michael's Priory, a Victorian foundation, at one time a private school for girls but since the Second World War used mainly for concerts and philanthropic functions.

For sale were displayed a variety of exhibits, mainly the work of senior girls from Briscombe High School, some of whom were on duty as stall-keepers. Mr Bentley gave only brief attention to the flowers, pet dogs and ruined castles, landscapes, seascapes, sailing-boats on blue waters, all conventional exercises. Not bad but nothing remarkable, he decided, and moved on until he came to the last one, a small oil enclosed in a home-made frame and signed *'To Ariadne'*. A note in the catalogue took his fancy.

> *Number 40. 'Elfride Awaits'. Discipula mea! Diligenter Picturam Specta! 12 x 9 inches, oil on canvas. This simple Latin imperative, inscribed on the back of the frame and addressed to a female child, reads "My Pupil, Look Carefully at the Picture", and is thought to indicate a singular property attributed to this unfinished work. The writer was probably Christina Dunn (1898-1935?) sometime drawing mistress at the St Michael's Priory School. "Ariadne" to whom the work is dedicated, was presumably the pupil addressed.*

Mr Bentley had spent several years learning Latin and decided to obey the artist's curious injunction to give the picture careful attention. What "singular property" might it have, he wondered and screwed in his monocle better to see the detail.

The background was of varied greens, lights and darks, with streaks of sepia brown for the mass of trees and bushes. At first glance the configuration seemed to present a wild incoherent mass but the initial impression of impenetrable foliage began to separate into distinct objects. In spite of the relatively small canvas an array of natural growths became almost distinguishable by species and the scene gradually identified itself as a flat clearing dominated by a sundial and an oak tree. The tree sheltered a squat headstone on which the shapes of letters had been sketched to represent an inscription.

Mr Bentley asked himself why the deceased Miss Dunn had left it unfinished and, for that matter, what was unfinished about it? To his eye it appeared complete, with every part of the small canvas filled. Had the unknown secret of the painted grave proved too much for her tender nature?

"Too much for mine, anyway", remarked Mr Bentley. "I don't fancy hanging that in my apartment" but when he went to treat himself to the English luxury of afternoon tea he began to have a guilty feeling on account of his failure to buy anything so he strolled back and inspected the painting again.

Pausing a short distance away he noticed that not only had the greenery become less opaque but also that something fresh had come into view. The cloaked figure of a woman carrying a spade was standing by the oak tree in the foreground while by the low gravestone a black hole was yawning eagerly as if waiting for an occupant. The stone was bathed in a faint greenish light while in the foreground, facing away from the observer, another woman and a young girl crouched, their faces turned away towards the apparition. One sensed their fear.

Such a grouping was common in late mediaeval European art, where the Grim Reaper, a sexless skeleton, usually carried a scythe, but to depict Death as a woman armed with any kind of implement was rare. Mr Bentley asked himself if it might have been objective, based upon an incident which the artist had actually observed or had she borrowed the image from one of those gloomy prints typical of the late Augustan "graveyard school"?

However, when he stood back a couple of paces the three figures had merged into a uniformly lush background. The green glow had gone and the painted surface of the stone bore only a series of illegible scratches.

"Now that's a cunning piece of work. One has to view it close-up. From the life, I'd say," murmured Mr Bentley, not realising the irony of his words. "It's original enough to be worth a few dollars".

One of the attendants, a thin worried-looking lady displaying a white label inscribed *Miss Eleanora Dellincourt* had been watching his close attention and came up to him nervously. She seemed unduly upset when he expressed his interest. Her lower lip trembled and her hollow cheeks paled.

"Oh dear," she said. "How did that thing get in! I thought it was destroyed after..." She broke off and swayed as though she were about to fall. Then she gathered herself up and looked Mr Bentley straight in the eye.

"No, sir, I'm sorry but this... er ... is definitely not for sale. It once belonged to a relative of mine and ... and it could bring ... bad luck. It ought to have an NFS label on it."

At that point a matronly *grande dame*, an elderly Queen Bee exuding a pervasive odour of authority, broke into the conversation. Her bright red label introduced her as Lady Felicity

Tarleton-Horrocks, recognised by the citizenry of Briscombe as a prominent patroness of the town's charitable functions.

"Ellie!" she trilled, "what is it that's not for sale? Is this gentleman showing an interest?"

Mr Bentley, sensing a conflict, introduced himself to both ladies rather disingenuously as a writer on art matters who would be grateful for any information they might give him on this particular work. It might, he said, make for an interesting article in *The Burlington Magazine*. Would they entertain an offer?

Mr Bentley was only an occasional subscriber to that distinguished journal but his air of dignified respectability and his transatlantic accent convinced Lady Tarleton-Horrocks that he was a visitor worthy of her full attention.

"Never mind what Ellie said. All the pictures here are for sale. We are running a charity after all. They're nearly all by local children. You won't find any masterpieces. This one is what I'd call a really dull effort. I'd have put it with the rubbish but with our showing this week I thought somebody might buy it."

On hearing this, Miss Dellingcourt paled and started to walk away, head down. Partly to cover her abject embarrassment and sensing a hidden undercurrent to which a stranger like himself was not privy, the sympathetic Mr Bentley offered five pounds, which Lady Tarleton-Horrocks accepted with alacrity, saying, "it is far too much for such a poor little daub, but thank you for your generosity ... and do go ahead and write your piece."

Mr Bentley, aware that his proposed article would never see the light of day, was beset by a stab of conscience.

"If you're not sure..." he began.

"Nonsense!" Lady Tarleton-Horrocks brushed aside his pretended objections. "Ellie, go and get a bag for the gentleman."

Having issued that clear instruction she took Mr Bentley aside and whispered. "*Entre nous*, I'm glad to see it go. It's got a bit of a history. There's a book by a local man that might help if you're going to write about it. We've a few copies left. Would you care to buy one?"

Without waiting for his response she escorted Mr Bentley to a stall offering second-hand books and produced a volume by a Major J.F. Stonor entitled *Briscombe and its Ghosts,* published only the year before. He handed over a shilling, thanked the strong-willed Lady Tarleton-Horrocks and made for the exit.

In a corner of the marquee he found a bench and sat down with the book. The Major had left few local ghosts undisturbed. Over the centuries phantoms had apparently made many appearances in and around Briscombe: Roman soldiers, white ladies, spectral dogs, headless horsemen and – inevitably in an area where so many religious houses had been founded – monks and nuns.

According to the industrious author, all these wraiths bar one were content to appear passively before the living. This singular exception was Sister Elfride, a nun of the ninth-century monastery dedicated to her namesake Saint Ethelfritha. In 1537 Sister Elfride had been excommunicated and her face burned off with red-hot irons before the mercy of hanging for the abduction and murder of the young daughter of a Catholic landowner, Sir Thomas Furneaux, in 1537. Henry VIII, newly broken away from Rome, had used this shocking example of perverted criminal conduct as a handy excuse for seizing the assets of the Abbey.

This outcast from the Papal Order had become a *revenant* or returner from the grave, bound for all eternity to haunt the Abbey gardens *without a face.* St Michael's Priory School was not founded until 1840 but even then, three centuries after the event, mothers still warned their female offspring not to enter the maze "lest the faceless nun got them". Occasional incidents involving persons of both sexes who claimed to have seen the faceless nun had added substance to the legend.

Mr Bentley did not believe in ghosts, certainly not actively oppressive ones. He consulted his gold pocket-watch. Ten past three. He would take time to visit this haunted garden. As he left the marquee a voice hailed him. It was Miss Dellincourt again. She had brought along his painting in a large brown paper bag and to his surprise and puzzlement, offered to buy it back for twice the price he had given Lady Felicity.

Sensing that there was much that he had not been told, Mr Bentley politely declined. He would need the painting for his article, he told her. Miss Dellincourt grasped his arm and repeated her earlier caution against bad luck. Mr Bentley, not a little irritated by her persistence, informed the lady that he would take the chance whereupon she tried another tack.

"Sir, if you are going to explore the Ancient Garden and the Maze, do take care that you don't lose your way. Keep to the paths. People might take advantage of a visitor like yourself. We often have trouble with diddicoys and suchlike."

Mr Bentley had never met with that expression in the United States, but he had a good idea what it meant.

"Don't worry Madam, I'll walk softly and carry a big stick, as Teddy Roosevelt said…"

"That wouldn't help you if you met…"

"Who? Sister Elfride?" he returned jocularly. "I'd speak to her nicely and ask her out to an English tea, like any civilized man."

"She may not be the only one…" murmured Miss Dellincourt, unsmilingly, and turned away. "There are other phantom dwellers…"

'By jiminy,' thought Mr Bentley, 'they do take their ghosts seriously around here.' Perceiving that the rain had stopped, he circled the edge of a wide playing field on which a herd of goats was feeding and found the entrance to the garden, a wooden gate hanging from its hinges. The dilapidated aviary no longer housed any birds. A track led a dozen yards past the aviary to a painted sign indicating 'The Maze'.

'This must be the place of ill-repute mentioned in Stonor's book,' he said to himself. Since exploring Hampton Court on a guided tour earlier that summer he had been attracted by the prospect of losing himself in a maze. Might this one be in a decent state of preservation?

It was not. Although he tried to stay on the path, he soon lost his way in its successive overgrown corners and tried to recall the classic formula for escape from the labyrinth at Hampton Court. Was the secret to keep turning left in alternate lanes and eventually one would emerge? Or was it first right and then left to get to the centre?

Mr Bentley had forgotten that particular escape route but in any event the Priory's maze had been long neglected and the key to its puzzle could no longer be interpreted in terms of any Tudor designer's plan. The dividing hedges hung carelessly over the weed-infested pathways and badly needed cutting back. The area covered by the twisting and turning routes was more extensive than Mr Bentley had expected and he could trace no regular pattern in its design. He became aware of a disquieting feeling that he personally had drawn down the attention of unwholesome if not unholy forces. He could sense an alien element all around him. This garden certainly was no haven of peace. Sunlight hardly penetrated the nooks and crannies of the criss-cross paths. He could almost swallow the tale of the waiting nun and began to regret his remark to Miss Dellingcourt.

By sheer hazard he at last emerged into what had to be the centre, an open patch of long grass, dotted here and there by clumps of nettles. He recognised it immediately. There stood the sundial and the massive trunk of the oak, its interior hollowed by age. He almost expected to see the open pit and the inscribed headstone but the ground under the massive tree lay undisturbed. Mr Bentley's gaze wandered slowly around the clearing and abruptly came to a stop.

He was standing on the exact spot where Christina Dunn had placed the figures confronted by the cloaked woman. Was her depiction supposed to represent an actual meeting with the ghostly nun Elfride? Had this terrible apparition really appeared to her and her pupil or had the chosen title been merely fanciful, derived from local superstition?

He extracted his purchase from the bag and compared it with the scene before him. A wave of excitement swept over him. Here was something new! The headstone and the open grave had reappeared on the canvas and this time an inscription was plainly legible:

She Awaits Thee In Our Garden.

Awaits thee? The grave's future occupant? Perhaps this implied question explained what was "unfinished" about it? In that case "Thee" must refer to himself. He had a sudden uncomfortable notion who the patient 'She' might be. Should he have taken the agitated Miss Dellincourt more seriously?

For a moment he took his eyes from the canvas. When he looked again he saw only the green background. The rain started to cascade down again, rattling incessantly on the leaves. He had no brolly. That settled matters.

"Baloney!" he muttered to himself. "Ghostly nuns, changing pictures, haunted mazes! I guess I need a drink".

He would return to the Crown and find solace in the bar.

In that moment Mr Bentley realised that something or someone was coming down one of the weed-strewn paths leading to the centre of the maze. At first he thought it was an animal, one of the goats grazing in the field that had strayed into the garden, but Mr Bentley, away from the City and unused to the ways of wildlife, on second thoughts decided that the sounds might well herald the appearance of a rural footpad, a "diddycoy" out to prey on an unwary visitor rash enough to enter the maze alone.

Mr Bentley was understandably unwilling to meet such a predator. He stumbled back the way he thought he had come and blundered around one blind corner after another, heading in what he was sure was the direction of the entrance. Untended growths of vine barred his clumsy progress, stretching out snake-like to impede him.

Abruptly he halted. The sounds had ceased. Good and bad both. No ruffian but he had managed to lose himself. What an fool he was, fleeing nervously from mere noises. He was unlikely to be the only person exploring the maze.

Later he was to persuade himself that he had been mistaken, deceived by another optical illusion but at the next corner stood the figure of a woman swathed in a long garment surmounted by a hood which came to an unpleasant point at the top. The woman raised her head. She had no face. Beyond the opening of the hood was nothing but a black empty space.

Mr Bentley did not stop to determine whether this was a human visitor playing a practical joke or an unearthly visitant from the grave. With a strangled cry he stumbled awkwardly away and started to run.

In his youth a useful sprinter, Mr Bentley was sadly unable to cover the ground with anything like the agility of his former athletic self, though his performance under pressure on unfamiliar ground was not to be despised. It was the urgent combination of more haste and less speed that brought him down. He tripped and went sprawling on the damp grass. A sharp stone pierced his ankle and he felt a stabbing pain in his chest. Fear forced him to scramble up and struggle on, but right away he came up against a dead end of twigs and branches stretching right across his path. He turned back the way he had come but found himself blocked again, this time by a mountain of greenery.

Once or twice in his life Mr Bentley had resigned himself to meet an ignominious end. Now this fatalistic conviction descended on him for the first time in years. He could hear his heart thumping. His doctor had cautioned him against strenuous exercise. He had to stop.

An uncanny silence had descended on the garden. The numbing constriction in his chest gradually subsided. His anxiety lessened and he was berating himself for his lapse into such undignified conduct when a dark shadow loomed on the other side of the green curtain.

A strangled cry broke from his lips, but it was not the ghastly faceless creature but a slightly-built girl in an old-fashioned grey linen frock and a whitish mob cap who drifted into his line of sight through a gap in the mass of greenery. He contemplated her for a moment and decided that she could not be a ghost. Perhaps she knew the quickest way out of this wretched place! He cleared his throat.

"Sorry about this, young lady. Stupid of me. But I'd be much obliged to you for some help. I'm completely lost. What's your name? I'm Charles, Charles Bentley. I'm from America, California."

Silently the other beckoned him to follow her into a gap which opened into a wide path. The confusion of greenery had cleared the path leading directly to the exit. How on earth could he have failed to notice it in his frantic race to escape. His guide still did not speak but ran ahead. No, she didn't exactly *run* – he sought for an exact word – she *flitted* along the grassy lane and he could have sworn that her feet hardly touched the ground.

His brain registered something strange about her movements. Didn't she look – slightly transparent? Surely he could see the shapes of the greenery *right through* her? His recent experience had left him open to the wildest of light-headed speculations. Was she a phantom after all? Didn't courtesy demand that one addressed a ghost by its name?

The signature on Christina's painting had dedicated the work to Ariadne, the beautiful daughter of King Minos who had shown Theseus how to escape from the deadly Cretan labyrinth after he had killed the Minotaur. Surely this attractive adolescent was helping him to evade a monster! Sure, he'd call her Ariadne.

Just as this whimsy occurred to him he spotted the derelict aviary looming ahead. Although he moved slowly, she had always stayed within his range of vision. He'd never have found the route alone. He would give her a sixpence.

Trudging on, Mr Bentley dwelt briefly on the absurdity of re-warding a ghost with a paltry coin of the realm. But Ariadne was no longer to be seen ahead of him. He had not noticed the exact moment when the diminutive figure had vanished. She must have flitted into some other hidden byway and melted into the green wall. He was sorry not have been able to thank her and make sure that she got home.

At last he pushed the gate open and found himself safely out of the Ancient Garden. It was then that he realised that he no longer carried the painting. He must have dropped it in his flight. He had no inclination to retrace his steps to look for it.

He limped across the playing-field and past the marquee. Mentally drained and physically fatigued he decided that on balance he didn't care much about the loss of 'Elfride Awaits'.

After all, it was really no more than a crude representation of the central area with some curious light and shade effects.

By the entrance to the tent he recognised the spare figure of Miss Eleanora Dellincourt and wondered if he ought to tell her that her warning of "phantom dwellers" had been completely justified but she turned away. Curiosity made him linger to see if anyone – a woman or a young girl – might come across the playing field from the direction of the Ancient Garden. He was relieved when no-one did.

A taxi deposited him at the Crown in time for a drink and a short fitful sleep after which he felt sufficiently recovered to face the rest of the day. He returned to Major Stonor's book and found three reproductions from the *Briscombe Reporter* of June 1935: the first showed a pretty child with dark hair wearing a school uniform and a straw boater, the second a fair-haired woman seated with a group of children similarly attired. She was swathed in a black academic gown. He shivered. He had seen something like it that very afternoon, though its wearer on that occasion, he told himself, was not from the land of the living. The child seated next to her teacher resembled the one in the first picture, but she was definitely not the young person to whom his heightened inspiration had given the name Ariadne. The girl in the maze had been several years older.

An accompanying caption, *"Teacher and pupil missing"* referred to Miss Christina Dunn and Alicia DeLancey, aged ten, who had not been seen for over a week. Could there possibly be a connection between the sinister apparition Mr Bentley had encountered in the garden and their disappearances several years before? An alarming answer readily occurred to him.

The third extract, was dated twelve months earlier and headed *Tragic Death of Miss Olivia Dellincourt.* Apparently she had been Head Mistress of the Priory School, found dead after a fire at the

School House and survived by her younger sister Eleanora, Latin mistress in the School for the past fifteen years.

Mr Bentley decided that if he were to find out more he must talk to the Major in person, if he was available. He was. From the slim telephone directory he learned that this gentleman lived at Owl-Tree Cottage, Rugeley Road, Little Briscombe and a telephone call indicated that Mr Bentley would be most welcome, next evening at six, in time for a "chota peg" and a chat about local ghosts.

The following day was wet and miserable so until late afternoon Mr Bentley confined himself to the hotel to finish the Major's book, which tailed off into a series of accounts by elderly folk who claimed to have experience of the supernatural in a number of its manifestations within thirty miles of Briscombe. Mr Bentley found it hard to credit most of their tales but at the same time doubted if the Major's contributors would consider his own adventure any more worthy of inclusion than their own.

The Major, an overweight pipe-smoker in his early sixties, occupied a red-roofed cottage that might have been a feature of a retirement magazine. It even had red roses growing in bunches around the door. Mr Bentley apologised for his intrusion and was told that the Major didn't meet many Americans but was always glad to welcome visitors "of the right sort", as he put it. Mr Bentley obviously fell marginally into that category.

In a study crammed with books and overseen by regimental photographs he was soon put at ease with the help of libations from a half-empty decanter of whisky. The Major puffed at his pipe and filled several pages with scribbled notes as Mr Bentley recited his un-nerving adventures in the Ancient Garden which his host attributed to his brief possession of Christina Dunn's curious work of art.

"Very interesting, old man. You've had a rare encounter. Most of the stories I get are hard to credit but yours rings true. You may have had a close shave. If you hadn't dropped the painting…"

"Was that the nun?" asked Mr Bentley but the Major did not answer directly. "I can fill you in only up to a point," he said. "You have to go back four years to the day when the Old School House was burned to the ground and Miss Olivia Dellincourt died in the fire. Eleanora Dellincourt inherited the Priory School from her sister and took over as Head Mistress."

The Major's pipe had gone out. He paused to relight it and to replenish his glass. Mr Bentley waited impatiently.

"After Christina Dunn and her pupil disappeared Miss Eleanora Dellincourt acquired the 'Elfride' painting. After all, Christina had been her colleague and it was left in a classroom.

"That's when I started to collect material for my book. There was plenty to write about, but I found that picture a promising leading subject. It's not especially well done but people said it was prophetic. Christina predicted her own meeting with the bogey in the garden. It was odd that she put the child in the scene. Did you know that the paint wasn't dry when it was discovered sitting on her easel? There were all kinds of explanations but the notion that this spook from Tudor times got them both didn't go down with the police. They wanted a quick arrest but that had to wait till the bodies turned up, which at the time they didn't."

The Major produced a copy of *Briscombe and Its Ghosts.*

"Look at these pictures from the *Reporter*. See here? That's Miss Olivia Dellincourt, the redoubtable Head Mistress herself. A good likeness. In her day quite a beauty. Compared with her Eleanora was an ugly duckling. Never managed to land a man. Olivia never married either but she was rumoured to have been a very good friend," he grinned in a conspiratorial fashion, "to Sir

Everard DeLancey Tarleton-Horrocks, a hard-up scion of the old Briscombe squirearchy. Everard died on active service in India in 1924. I knew him fairly well. Fellow got himself hitched on his last leave, but not to Olivia. I gather you met his widow, the Lady Felicity. Moneybags. Eleanora's right under her thumb."

Major Stonor poured himself another Scotch and confirmed his guest's developing suspicions. "Everybody guessed that Alicia DeLancey was Olivia's illegitimate daughter, aged ten when she vanished with her teacher Christina Dunn. The *Reporter* alleged that they must have fallen into the clutches of "the faceless nun". When the War started in 1939 the Government requisitioned the buildings and used them to house internees detained under Regulation 18B. It was never re-opened as a school.

"There's a lot I haven't told you. I'm saving it for the second edition of my book. My advice in the meantime is to stay away from the Priory grounds and take the next train back to London. I've done enough research on our local hauntings to convince me that it's unwise to dismiss them all out of hand. More things in heaven and earth, old man. After your trip to the woods I'm sure you won't disagree. As for the long-deceased Christina's so-called work of art, my advice is to forget you ever saw it."

With that the Major drained his glass and climbed unsteadily to his feet. The interview was over. Mr Bentley had him sign and date *Briscombe and Its Ghosts* and set off for the Crown Hotel just as dusk was gathering.

Mr Bentley returned to the United States and a year later the Second World War changed the face of Britain. He never set foot in Briscombe again but he did sometimes wonder if the Major had ever brought out his second edition and one day placed an order for a copy through a New York agency.

Time passed and he had almost forgotten about his request when a slim volume entitled *The Grisly Secret of 'Elfride Awaits'* and enclosing a bill was delivered to his ocean apartment with apologies for delay in filling his order on account of the change of title and the postponement of publication owing to the death of its author two years earlier.

Mr Bentley did not need more than a cursory inspection of his purchase to realise that the Major's original emphasis on local superstitions had been completely overshadowed by a creative-fictional account of Briscombe's sensational murder case. He had not heard of such a murder, but Briscombe's crimes did not rate much attention in San Francisco, which had plenty of her own.

At first he was disappointed to learn that the deceased Major had been less than honest. Mr Bentley's account of his own brief stewardship of Christina's painting and of that terrifying after-noon in the Ancient Garden had been dramatically incorporated into one of the early chapters without the slightest acknowl-edgement of the American's part in it. The faceless nun legend was given a fresh lease of life, with Major Stonor citing an un-named witness.

That irritated Mr Bentley but at his age he saw no advantage in pursuing the unscrupulous Major beyond the grave, an area he preferred to avoid. In fact, by the time he had finished reading, he had become grateful to the sodden old dug-out for leaving the name of Bentley out of his narrative.

The Major's second edition provided a racy version of facts and speculations surrounding the murder and contained some familiar names. In 1946 German prisoners were mustered to erect pre-fabricated houses on the Priory site. By then the maze had fallen into a sorry state of neglect. Most of what remained of it was cut down and the ground dug over. Several of the prisoners reported a strange presence within the Ancient Garden area and refused to work there.

Dissent came to a head when two skeletons were disinterred by one of the less impressionable Germans. In the same grave was found a bloodstained spade. A small painting wrapped in sackcloth was uncovered from within the trunk of a hollow oak in what had been the centre of the maze. From dental records the remains were identified as those of Christina Dunn and Alicia deLancey. The police arrested Eleanora Dellincourt, then in her fifties, and linked her to a strong motive.

On taking over the administration of the School after Olivia's death, Eleanora had discovered a birth-certificate proving that her elder sister Olivia had given birth to a baby girl, Alicia. She had also found a late will of Olivia's, bequeathing all she possessed "to my love-child, Alicia deLancey", whose natural father was not named.

The provisions of the will were unusual. If Alicia failed to attain her majority the entire estate, including the Priory School, was to descend, not to the expectant sister Eleanora, but to Lady Felicity Tarleton-Horrocks, "relict of Captain Sir Everard De-Lancey Tarleton-Horrocks".

The Crown's case in *Rex v. Dellincourt* rested on the argument that the dispossessed and violently jealous Eleanora had lured Alicia into the maze and killed her with the spade. Christina Dunn had by chance witnessed this horrific murder of one of her pupils, a crime which she had predicted in the last of her own paintings. Eleanora allegedly killed her too and buried the two corpses under the oak-tree along with the bloodstained weapon. Mr Bentley now understood why Lady Felicity's contribution to the exhibition of Christina's prophetic painting had given her such a nasty shock and made her unwilling to see it sold to a stranger who proposed to write an article about it.

Eleanor pleaded Not Guilty to both murders but insisted that she did not hide the painting, which had been sold in an exhibition of child art before the war. Lady Felicity Tarleton-Horrocks, aged eighty, called as a witness, had no idea who had bought it but "the man said he was going to write an article about it for some artistic magazine". Mr Bentley was glad that he had not been able to keep his promise to Lady Felicity. He had a good excuse.

In a statement, read out in court, the accused alleged that in June 1935 the two victims had gone to keep a rendezvous with Sister Elfride in the Ancient Garden. It was Elfride, not herself, whom Christina Dunn had painted carrying the lethal spade. It was Elfride, not herself, who had murdered them. Did they know that it was with a spade that the nun had killed the fifteen-year-old Ariadne Furneaux in 1537?

Ariadne? Now Mr Bentley understood. Christina had dedicated her painting to Elfride's original victim, not to her living pupil Alicia. Mr Bentley had met her himself, the semblance of the girl whom he had thought of as Ariadne, in life her real name. He wondered who or what had hidden his lost painting in the hollow trunk of the oak tree. Ariadne again? The Major had left out her part in Mr Bentley's story and Miss Dellincourt's statement had done little to persuade her counsel to accept *Elfride Awaits as* a significant item of evidence.

The case for the Defence was largely circumstantial and relied too heavily on the supernatural element to convince a hard-headed jury that Eleanora's confused version had any merit. She was found guilty but insane and committed to an asylum where she remained for twelve years. On her release, Lady Felicity, who had paid for her defence, offered her a position as companion. Malicious tongues wagged, but with such influential support Miss Eleanora was permitted, in the fullness of time, to rejoin the serried ranks of Briscombe society.

Following the trial *Elfride Awaits* had been listed in a London auction catalogue and bought by an unnamed client for fifteen hundred pounds.

13. *Three Weddings and Three Funerals*

Flora Watts and William Cudlipp worked in the same branch of a London suburban bank. From his late teens William, encouraged by his widowed mother, had acquired what might be called "intellectual interests" and was a regular film-, theatre- and concert-goer and a keen book collector. Flora pretended enthusiasm for all of these in the hope of luring him to the altar. She had been twice jilted and at the over-ripe age of thirty-eight was resolved not to miss what might well be her last chance of wedlock with a presentable suitor. But her belief in communication with the world beyond, regularly expressed in the dogma "Dead is not Dead" was something which William did not share.

As for William himself, his motives were different. He was tired of living at home with his widowed mother when most of his friends were married and had their own establishments. At thirty-four he decided to ignore her warnings against possible 'Jezebels' and casually proposed to Flora, a plain girl five years older than himself and in June of 1932 their nuptials were clumsily consummated in the bridal suite of an Eastbourne boarding-house – for better or worse.

The spirits ought to have warned Flora that they were to be for worse. William's salary as an accounts-clerk with prospects was just sufficient for their joint needs, without luxuries, and as in those days the Bank preferred not to employ married women, Flora resigned her cashier's position and set herself to concentrate on the office of housekeeping. William was promoted to 'securities' and transferred to a recently-opened branch in Surrey. The Bank favoured him with a low-interest loan and he bought a bungalow – Number 33, Lacey Avenue – in one of the fast-growing, Jerry-built developments within a short bus-ride of his new post.

Marriage and subsequent promotion changed William's life, but from his point-of-view not for the better. He could no longer afford to attend Old Vic plays or Queen's Hall concerts with the same regularity as before and now spent most Saturdays reading or listening to music on the Regional Programme while Flora went shopping or pored over her women's magazines. On Tuesday evenings she would go to a séance and on her return subject her husband to a recital of her latest encounter with the spirit world. "Remember, dead is not dead," she told him. "We will always be together and if I die before you, I will return."

Initial amusement led to boredom on his part and after sitting in on one séance, held in their own house, he told his wife's elderly guests that so far as he could make out they were all already dead. This tactless remark led to their first real quarrel. There were to be many others as time went on.

Another source of friction was William's mother, Millicent, who in the early days was a frequent visitor to Number 33. Flora resented her constant petty criticisms, while Millicent came to consider her daughter-in-law as domestically incompetent and her belief in spirits and the after-life an attribute of the grossly uneducated. Flora's parents Millicent considered "common" – working class, ignorant people who did not fit in with her *petit bourgeois* notions of what constituted "proper" behaviour. After a couple of disastrous weekend invitations Mr Watts told his daughter that they'd had enough of "that bloody snob" and in future would visit Number 33 only if they didn't have to meet her.

Things might have settled themselves had Flora produced a baby, but this didn't happen. In those days giving birth was not considered "safe" for a woman over forty. This suited William, himself an only child, who did not want a family. Flora tried to lavish her limited maternal instincts on a dog, but when the beast was run over, William, who disliked domestic pets, refused to let her replace it.

One perceptible change in Flora's day-to-day behaviour he found especially alarming. On the slightest pretext she would break into violent rages and exhaust herself in tearful recriminations. She started to complain of severe headaches which she called "migraines" and would maintain a moody silence for hours. William's attempts to get her to see a doctor were greeted with accusations that he was persecuting her, so he preferred to leave the house to avoid conflict. His chosen refuge was the local pub, *The Bird in Hand*.

One evening in *The Bird* William fell into conversation with an attractive widow, Mrs Hazel George, who had recently lost her husband, a well-to-do builder. From their very first encounter she made no secret of her attraction to William, a good-looking man whose interest in films and the theatre gave him an advantage over the other regulars in *The Bird*. He told her that he had been not long married to a woman who had no interest in the kind of films he liked. She replied that she hated going to the cinema alone and squeezed his hand. Flattered by her flirtatious attentions, William saw that Mrs George not only possessed an agreeable temperament but also a range of sociable traits which his own wife conspicuously lacked. Flora, brought up in a teetotal household, would never dream of entering a hostelry like *The Bird*. This circumstance allowed her husband's friendship with Mrs George to develop undetected and within a week "Hazel" had accepted "Bill's" invitation to a Saturday *matinee* at the Odeon cinema, where 'foreign' films were occasionally shown. They held hands in the back row of the stalls. William had told

Flora that the picture was an old German silent horror, confident that she would not seek to accompany him, nor did she – but one of Flora's spiritualist circle politely acknowledged William and his companion as he was buying the tickets. While the pair were engrossed in the speechless antics of the murderous Dr Caligari and in each other, William's mother Millicent, like her daughter's dog, became the victim of a fatal traffic accident and expired in a South London hospital aged sixty-seven. Her son did not find out until the next day when he was stricken by a combination of guilt and remorse. Flora shed no tears but at the funeral William broke down. At the next Tuesday séance a message came to Flora through a female medium in a deep bass voice intended for "the deceived wife of a gentleman not long married". Flora immediately identified this person with herself and asked her husband awkward questions, for which he had only awkward answers.

Like all soothsayers' warnings this one was equivocal. The actual words relayed by the medium were hardly novel. *"Cherchez la femme"* was a familiar phrase first recorded in the mid-eighteenth century. Though William did not know this gobbet of literary history and Flora had never studied French, both of them understood what the message implied.

The admonition was well-timed, for on the following Saturday disaster struck when William incautiously took Hazel to another film, followed by a couple of rounds in *The Bird*. This time they were spotted emerging hand in hand by Flora's hairdresser, another fellow-spiritualist and *confidante*, who regarded it as a bounden duty to report the observation to her client. This confirmed Flora's suspicions. A blazing row ended in blows which led to William's flight and permanent banishment to the spare bedroom. He showed Hazel the bruise on his head where Flora had hit him with the handle of her umbrella. Hazel responded sympathetically, assuring him that if he were her husband things would be very different.

William was not slow to appreciate the purport of this unsubtle hint and its particular significance for him. Statistics on longevity gathered by insurance companies indicated that women lived longer then men so that Flora might easily survive him. He was nearly thirty-six. The prospect of an interminable future with Flora was beginning to weigh heavily on him and bliss with a wife like Hazel beckoned more and more.

In those recent but relatively unenlightened times, divorce was expensive and rare among members of the lower middle classes, whose puritan traditions stood against concocted evidence of adultery and embarrassing reportage in a certain notorious scandal-sheet. The appearance of respectability was what mattered, a fact which made co-habitation without benefit of clergy unwise and socially unacceptable. Mr Poole, William's godlike Bank Manager, would never tolerate an employee engaged in what was then referred to as "living in sin". Besides, William could not afford to support a second home. He naturally thought of murder as a quick solution, but knew he would never have the nerve. Hazel, who enthusiastically became his mistress on the Friday following William's incandescent row with Flora, made a more constructive suggestion, namely, that he should immediately resign from the Bank and live with her in *Lamorna*, the ugly late Victorian mansion which she had inherited from Mr Maurice George.

William rapidly weighed up the pros and cons. He realised that he was never to attain the giddy heights of senior-managership and that he was destined to stay in the same post, advanced by small promotions within his grade until he was fifty-five. His prospects were secure but uninspiring. In nineteen more years he could retire and with the Bank's loan fully repaid, live unhappily ever after with Flora at his side.

The choice was not a difficult one and a decision was quickly reached. He made up his mind to burn his boats and sent up a letter of resignation, which Mr Poole reluctantly accepted. On the same day he told Flora that he was leaving her and would remove his personal belongings to *Lamorna*. She could keep the house and furniture, Hazel would redeem his debt to the Bank and he would pay off the mortgage.

Another very unpleasant scene followed in which expressions like "kept man" and "gigolo" were flung at his head. Flora was to show him a spiteful, vindictive side of her character. When William turned up at Number 33 with a light van to collect his portable property he ran the gauntlet of more verbal abuse and found that she had slashed his suits and shirts with a razor, given away his stamp-collection and poured ink on many of his most prized books. Not content with causing material damage she had also sent a rambling letter to the Bank's Head Office and even called at the Branch in person, describing in detail within earshot of staff and customers what her unfaithful husband had done to her and their marriage. Mr Poole tactfully sympathised with her unhappy position as the wife betrayed, but since both she and William had resigned, sympathy was all that the Branch Manager could offer. Flora even confronted "that rich bitch" Hazel in the street, screaming insults and curses.

Where all this might have ended was never to be known for Flora was to be diagnosed with a fast-developing brain tumour about which, at that time, medical science was relatively uninformed. A conscience-stricken William, realising the sad cause of her tantrums, visited her hospital bed daily and endured the baleful stare and silent accusation which accompanied her last weeks. He tried to tell her how sorry he was and that when she recovered all would be restored but he knew and she knew that his words were empty. Hazel had replaced her in almost every respect and when one afternoon he was summoned to the hospital at short notice and told that his wife was unlikely to last out the night his only genuine emotion was relief. Flora's last coherent words to him were cryptic. "Dead is not dead". She soon relapsed into a coma and expired without recovering consciousness.

A week later William stood, head bowed, as a callow young clergyman from St Jude's Presbyterian Church intoned the dire words "*earth to earth, ashes to ashes, dust to dust in sure and certain hope of the Resurrection unto eternal life*" and watched as the oaken coffin was lowered into the pit, the *long home*, as the *Book of Ecclesiastes* called it. "Long", he knew, meant "permanent, a last resting-place for all eternity".

"Dead really is dead," he said to himself.

When the last clod of earth had rattled on the coffin lid he shook hands with those few non-spiritualist friends of Flora's who did not treat him as a pariah. On the following Sunday morning he went to church as an act of courtesy to the young minister who had conducted the funeral. The latter took his text from the *Book of Job*. The verse "*Thou shalt come to thy grave in a full age, like as a shock of corn cometh in a full season*" promised William much more time on earth in a happier condition.

To ease his conscience he had several honeymoon photographs of Flora and himself enlarged and framed. In accord with prevailing local regulations he had to let a year pass before a small granite headstone might be erected on the grave. He inscribed it with a line from a Shakespeare sonnet.

> *FLORA ELIZABETH,*
> *DEARLY BELOVED WIFE*
> *OF WILLIAM CUDLIPP*

BORN DECEMBER 28th 1893
DIED JANUARY 16th 1934

"Love is not love which alters when it alteration finds"

William tried not to dwell on the more unpleasant details of the physical process which such alteration involved and began to wish he had thought of a different quotation when he placed the order. It occurred to him that "Love is not Love" had the same ring as "Dead is not Dead".

Every Saturday afternoon he trudged the two miles to St Jude's churchyard and arranged a fresh spray of roses on Flora's grave. He repeatedly suffered spasms of anguish and wished fervently that his last months with Flora had not been blighted by those terrible rows. Moreover, he could not rid himself of a nagging feeling that her illness might have been brought on partly by his treatment of her.

Hazel proposed marriage, but at first he held back, affected by an unreasonable fear which he could not identify. But Hazel was impatient and insistent so that after a Registry Office ceremony with witnesses drawn from passers-by Mrs George became the second Mrs Cudlipp only three months after Flora's passing. She arranged their honeymoon, not to a boarding-house in an English seaside resort but to an expensive hotel in Paris. William had never been abroad before and the experience invigorated him. He returned to England with a fresh appetite for the pleasures of living once again as a married man in Hazel's considerably more imposing residence. He sold Number 33, learned to drive and bought a car to take her for weekend spins into the country.

From her first husband Hazel had inherited a Parsee couple named Richards as cook-housekeeper and gardener, luxuries denied to William on a bank clerk's salary. William entered into his second term of matrimony confident that fortune had really come his way but still haunted by the uneasy memory of his first wife's last words.

References to Flora in conversation were regarded by Hazel as taboo. She removed the framed photographs of his first honeymoon with the snappish comment "Dead is dead. Remember I'm your wife now and very much alive," and threw them in the dustbin. William made no open objection. He did not dare to upset her and hastened to reassure her when she sought confirmation, which was often, that his romantic feelings for her had not abated.

Hazel made sure that the Richardses earned their wages. *Lamorna*, a largish property at the edge of the Green Belt, was well maintained inside and out and William himself was not expected to help. He took up golf and drove Hazel up to London to attend the latest plays. In those idyllic times, ownership of a motor vehicle was a luxury and the roads leading to the capital were almost empty. He had become a complete man of leisure and told himself that there was no reason why he should not be supremely happy. Yet even Eden had its serpent.

Hazel had expressed her disapproval of the churchyard visits so William gave Cyril, the gardener at St Jude's, a handsome renewable tip to maintain the plot until further notice with a regular spray of cut flowers. He decided that he would not continue to keep up the ritual himself. The image of Flora's malign deathbed scowl would not go away.

After William had enjoyed his new life of ease for a year, the memorial headstone was finished and erected, bearing the line from *Sonnet 116* which he had had ordered, inscribed in gilt letters. He could not help noticing that from the very day when the masons raised the headstone in his presence, unpleasant dreams began to interfere with his sleep. Most of them eluded his waking memory but there was one exception, a particularly frightening vision, in which he was carrying his floral offering, transformed into a bouquet of lilies, along a crabbed maze of rough pathways but lost his bearings and wandered about the cemetery from one grave plot to the next in increasing desperation with the bouquet becoming heavier and heavier until he could hardly support its leaden weight. At last he found his way barred by an enormous monument looming out of a thick reddish mist and in the dream dropped the flowers to find himself in their bedroom at home, with Hazel lying dead on the floor and Flora leaning over him, grinning, her face half-hidden in a white shroud. Somehow her corpse had got out of the grave and into their house. "Oh no, please go away," he muttered as he emerged from the first horror and was drawn helplessly screaming into the second.

Hazel demanded to know what was wrong. When he told her that he was plagued by hideous nightmares involving a vengeful Flora, she ridiculed him. She had no patience with such absurd premonitions. Seeing his distress, she turned it into a joke.

"That ghastly woman must be mouldering by this time. After all it's been well over a year. She'd better not turn up here!"

William lacked the assured scepticism which he once had, but in the secure comfort of *Lamorna* managed to subdue his fears and laugh with her. Next afternoon, after a heavy lunch, he drifted off to sleep in front of the fire and was rapidly transported to that same burial place with such clarity as to persuade him that he was actually there. All at once the familiar headstone appeared at the very end of a treeless path which ended at a wall. This was not its usual position but William accepted the displacement. He was normally rather short-sighted but in his dream state he could see from a distance that the surface of the stone displayed a different line, not in gold, but in black.

FLORA ELIZABETH
How long will a woman lie in the earth ere she rot?

In his dream he knew it for a misquotation from Shakespeare. Straining his eyes to read it, he sensed a grip on his shoulder. He was in the midst of another nightmare. Struggling to free himself he awoke shivering in front of the fire. He realised that he must not dwell in the past. Hazel was right. Dead was indeed dead and life was for the living. It was time to move on but first he just had to visit the real-life scene in daylight. These interruptions to his slumbers were only figments drawn from his past, called by his favourite poet "insubstantial pageants", He would go to St Jude's one last time to bid Flora farewell and to be sure that the gravestone was as it should be. That inscription carried with it a worrying reality and try as he would he could not expel Hazel's image of a mouldering body from his thoughts.

Hazel herself had gone upstairs for her afternoon sleep and he saw no reason to disturb her with unnecessary explanations which could only cause friction. He ran the car out quietly and followed the familiar route, stopping as usual at the corner florist from whom he bought an extra large bouquet of roses and chrysanthemums. Walking up the gravel path at the churchyard he was relieved to find the grave undisturbed. Why shouldn't it be? The original gilt lettering was plain to see. What Freudian rubbish one comes across in dreams, he thought and kneeling, placed his large floral token on the ground beside the new headstone.

"Goodbye Flora", he whispered. "Forgive me. Hazel won't let me come here again".

As he spoke the flowers seemed to wither away and the memorial stone toppled backwards. The grave burst open and something greyish and damp smelling rose out of the hole. A mottled face half-concealed by a semi-transparent veil loomed over him. A lipless mouth gaped in an obscene parody of a kiss.

He told himself that this could not be, that this grisly apparition was no more than a projection of his own guilty conscience. *Love is not love which alters when* it *alteration finds.* Dead is dead. How could he ever associate that repulsive veiled horror with Flora though common sense told him that she probably did look like that after burial for the best part of two years. *How long will a man lie i' the earth ere he rot?* Hamlet should have asked the garrulous gravedigger about a woman? Perhaps they lasted longer?

William retched . Was this her revenge? Could the dead still menace the living world from beyond the grave?

"I didn't realise … I'm sorry Flora," he babbled. "Sorry, sorry, sorry…" Now wide awake, he was vomiting on the wet ground.

An elderly man sporting the plus-fours fashionable at the time and leading a large Alsatian dog stopped when he saw William.

"Are you all right? You look ill. Can I help you? You'd best sit down. There's a seat over there."

He grasped William's arm. William flinched and shouted hysterically. The dog growled and glared menacingly at this seeming threat to his owner, who pulled him back.

"It's all right, he doesn't bite. Please sit down!"

A group of people bearing flowers was gathering, attracted by the commotion and curious to discover what was disturbing the trembling man. Had he been attacked?

William collapsed on the wooden bench and sawed the air with wild gestures, mouth opening and shutting as he struggled to breathe.

"My wife's grave … no, my first wife … it's open and … she … no … not her … it was something … came out!"

He could not reconcile the two images – the woman he remembered and the shrouded, bony, fetid corpse with the ruined,
almost but not wholly unrecognisable face which had reared up
out of her grave.

A formidable-looking man said he was an off-duty police officer. He assumed that vandals had been despoiling the memorials.
The rest he put down to a recently bereaved husband's distress.
He asked William to show him the place and took him by the
arm.

"Along here is it sir? Not far along you say? I don't see anything. Are you sure this is the right path sir? No I'm not
doubting you did see some kind of an upheaval – they've been
digging and leaving mounds of earth. Ah, here it is, Flora Eliza-
beth. Is that your wife's name? It's your first wife? No damage.
Look and see for yourself sir."

William looked and looked again. There was the granite headstone, its original gilt lettering intact. The earth was undisturbed.
His bouquet was fresh and lying where he had placed it.

A dazed William spent hours at the police station repeating his
bizarre story. Eventually the police drove him back home to find
an ambulance blocking the drive and a shocked Richards hardly
able to stand up. Mrs Richards calmly told them that she had
found Mrs Cudlipp "falling down". She'd called their doctor and
the ambulance. "The doctor said mistress had suffered a heart-
attack."

Hazel was slumped on the hall floor, her features chalk-white,
her gaze fixed on vacancy. Lumps of earth were scattered on the
carpet. Two St John's ambulance men regarded him silently and
with distrust. The police officers who had brought him back
prepared to escort him away again "to help with enquiries".

His story would not have been believed had the case ever
come to the Assizes, but William had a well-supported alibi

which could not be upset. Statements taken from the Richardses confirmed that Mr William Cudlipp had left *Lamorna* in his car alone and that Mrs Hazel Cudlipp was resting in her bedroom when he drove off. Richards himself said he was digging at the rear of the property when he saw a strange woman gliding up the path towards the back door.

"Yes sir, I understand, gliding is what I said exactly. A long dress she was wearing. Her feet I am not seeing. Is she knocking on the front door really? Why else would she have gone that way? But I am seeing nobody at all coming out Ask my wife."

Mrs Victoria Richards was in the kitchen listening to music on the wireless when she had looked out of the window and seen this "trespasser person" approaching the house from the wood at the back. "I fancied she was a poor person coming begging really, always wearing a long grey frock and her face hiding in a veil. No doorbell ringing. Not a single sound of any live person entering actually. I go outside to look but she was gone again. At half-past three I take the mistress afternoon tea and there she was down falling unconscious in the hall so I call ambulance."

Mrs Richards could not explain the presence of earth-droppings in the hall unless Richards had brought it in on his boots which was unlikely since she had hoovered the hall only that morning and also her husband was not allowed in that part of the house. In her opinion (laughing) it was a ghost only. The county coroner reprimanded her but the London *Evening Standard* picked up her comment and made a headline out of it. A post-mortem reported cardiac arrest, though Mrs Cudlipp had no record of heart-trouble. Suspicion of William's role in the tragedy at first clouded the coroner's judgment. To him it did not seem normal behaviour for any man in his right mind to run away from an absurd daydream involving the fancied resurrection of his first wife while his second wife lay dead or dying at their home two miles away, but his court was unable to establish a connection. William pleaded that the grave be reopened to make certain that it still contained a body. His incredible tale was considered a fantasy but confirmation of the time element convinced the coroner's jury that on the evidence available Mr William Cudlipp could not have been responsible for whatever happened to his wife and that a verdict of death from natural causes was the only one appropriate. The strange "trespasser person" who "glided" into the garden at *Lamorna* failed to respond to a police request to come forward. William's lawyer's appeal for an exhumation order was rejected.

In due course William inherited *Lamorna* and the bulk of Hazel's estate. He had her body cremated, sold *Lamorna* and went to live in South Africa where he was married again within a year – this time to a psychiatric nurse.

~ E N D ~